TELLING STORIES TO CHILDREN

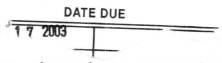

DATE DUE

1 7 2003

Once upon a time, so the story goes, people who loved children effortlessly told them bedtime stores. They had all the time in the world to dream up exciting plots, enchanting characters and wise morals. Everyone was a gifted storyteller. But no longer. Today, so we assume, storytelling cannot be done as it was before.

The truth is rather different. Telling stories to children has never been easier or more rewarding than it can be today. Everyone can learn how to entertain, inform and enjoy children through stories.

Here, in practical, easy-to-follow steps, father and bedtime storyteller Marshall Shelley discusses what makes a story good, where to get ideas, how to keep children's interest, ways to build drama and heighten suspense...and much more.

Throughout the book, you will find a variety of inspiring story-starters—ideas and plots certain to spark stories of your own.

Telling stories is one of the best possible ways to entertain, educate, stimulate creativity, reassure, and have fun with children. Who could ask for a happier ending than that?

Marshall Shelley is editor of *Leadership* magazine. His published books include *The Healthy, Hectic Home* and *Well-Intentioned Dragons*. He and his wife, Susan, live with their daughters, Stacey, Kelsey and Mandy, in Wheaton, Illinois.

W9-CGL-069

*To Stacey, Kelsey and Mandy, who've heard, inspired and
contributed to most of these tales*

Telling Stories to Children

Marshall Shelley

A LION PAPERBACK
Oxford · Batavia · Sydney

50,885   8-91   7.95

Published by
Lion Publishing Corporation
1705 Hubbard Avenue, Batavia, Illinois 60510, USA
ISBN 0 7459 1903 0
Lion Publishing plc
Sandy Lane West, Oxford, England
ISBN 0 7459 1903 0
Albatross Books Pty Ltd
PO Box 320, Sutherland, NSW 2232, Australia
ISBN 0 7324 0239 5

First edition 1990

Library of Congress Cataloging-in-Publication Data
Shelly, Marshall.
    Telling stories to children/Marshall Shelley — 1st ed.
    ISBN 0 7459 1903 0
    1. Storytelling. 2. Children—Books and reading. I. Title
Z718.3.S5 1990
027.62 51–dc20

British Library Cataloging in Publication Data
Shelley, Marshall
Telling stories to children.
    1. Children's stories. Story-telling
    I. Title
    372.64
    0-7459-1903-0

Printed in the United States of America

Contents

PART ONE

Wide-Eyed in Wonder

What story do you remember most vividly from childhood? What scenes still surface now, years later? Perhaps a knight in dread combat with a dragon. A frontiersman moving silently through the woods to rescue his friends. Or a young woman toiling as a chambermaid, unaware that she's really a princess.

From the earliest days of history, people have told stories. Through stories, people have kept alive the mighty deeds of ancient heroes and have engaged the imaginations of the younger generation. The position of the storyteller over the years has been an honorable one—kings and peasants alike would grant the storyteller their time, attention and occasionally their treasure. For centuries, stories provided entertainment, information and inspiration.

Gradually the role of the storyteller declined as books, newspapers and, later, electronic media gained prominence. Today, storytelling may be fading as a living art. The old tales, handed down orally for generations, are becoming more and more the preserve of the scholar.

Yet stories continue to be an influential, if sometimes overlooked, part of our lives. They are powerful, lingering long after the actual telling is over. The images stay in our minds. Beyond simply being good entertainment, stories inevitably help give our lives meaning. We identify with some characters and against others. Some of us root for knights; others, for dragons.

In a deeper sense, most of us—consciously or not—see our lives as being part of a larger story. Each of us faces conflict, obstacles, disappointment. We go on because we believe there's a chapter yet to be written; our present struggles will not be in vain.

This book is a tool to help parents with children at bedtime (or on long drives in a car). It's a tool for teachers with a class full of active little ones. It is for any adult who enjoys stories, who understands how impoverished we would be without them, and who wants to pass on the treasure of a story-fed imagination to the next generation.

Chapter 1

What Telling Stories Can Do

"Well, that's just a story." When I first heard that phrase, I suddenly realized that not everyone thinks stories are significant. To many people, stories are unimportant. They're not solid or substantial; they're fringe, embroidery. They don't deal with hard facts. They're not *real*.

To these people, stories serve the same function as pictures in a geography textbook. The facts are in the words—population, agricultural products, average rainfall—and the pictures are merely visual relief. But when you think of the word *Switzerland,* what comes to mind? Unless we've actually been there and have firsthand mental images, I would guess that the image most of us have is from a picture—the mighty Matterhorn, a yodeler, or cows grazing on a mountainside with a chalet nearby.

In one sense, stories *are* like pictures: they have lasting effect. They stay with us.

As I've thought about stories—and as I've told stories to my children at home and to classes of children in other settings—I've recognized the power of stories. Here are just a few of the things stories do.

Stories Feed the Mind and the Emotions

"The impact of the first things you read goes deep," says novelist Graham Greene. "A great part of the future is sitting on the shelves of libraries."

What's true of books is even more true of stories, because children will consume stories long before they're capable of reading books. Stories will help even the youngest children learn what to expect in life and how to interpret life's experiences.

A story in the mind of a child can have far-reaching consequences. "Childhood is the time of life when everything is awakening," says Genevieve Lejeune, who is responsible for "Children and Media," a program of the International Catholic Child Bureau. "Children absorb all that they find in their immediate environment. Their intelligence, their awareness, everything in them takes color from what they experience"—including the stories they're told by adults.

Stories Link Us to Life

Stories develop a common tradition, a frame of reference that's necessary to understand our world.

Storytelling requires at least two people. This sets it apart from other media. Watching television, for instance, is a solitary activity. Children can be mere inches from each other, but when absorbed in a TV show, they are often oblivious to one another (and to parents seeking their attention). Even reading a book, unless it's read aloud, is done alone.

Storytelling, however, is a shared experience. A relationship is established between teller and listener. A story cannot be told unless that relationship exists. Fortunately most children, when exposed to a comfortable setting and an exciting story, are eager to maintain that relationship.

As a result, stories create a common tradition. Both teller and listener experience something together. Together we climb the beanstalk with the boy named Jack, and together we tremble when he sees the ferocious giant. We learn that *Fe, fi, fo, fum* is a dread phrase. We know the relief that comes when Jack chops down the beanstalk before the giant is able to grind his bones for bread.

These common experiences strengthen the ties between adults and children. After enjoying stories together, we can speak the same language. When children talk about giants or fear or safety, we know how those words and concepts were learned. As adults, we can refer to stories that illustrate bravery or kindness and know that our children understand.

Stories help the generations communicate at a level deeper than mere words. They communicate concepts and values to young people in ways they can understand.

Stories Link Us to Our Past

Ours has been called "a cut-flower society." In an increasingly transient culture, we often find ourselves separated from our roots. For some children, grandparents are those folks you see once a year—if that often. Great-grandparents may be simply names on a family tree—if the family even bothers to keep one. Ethnic and religious backgrounds, in many cases, are lost in the leveling winds of mobility, mass media, and the shifting values of modern culture.

As they grow older, many young people struggle because they don't know where they came from. Cut free from their past, they find themselves adrift, lacking identity. Why is it so many adopted children sense a need to discover their birth mother? Why do so many others wonder, Who am I? What makes me unique?

Stories can answer those questions, and play an important role in shaping a child's identity, in at least two ways.

Stories can link us to our family. A little girl named Martha Taft once said, "My name is Martha Bowers Taft. My great-grandfather was president of the United States. My grandfather was a United States senator, my daddy is ambassador to Ireland, and I am a Brownie." You can bet her parents told her stories. And the lessons stayed with her.

11

We all want our children to know who they are. This means they not only know their heritage, but they know themselves. They feel their interests are worth mentioning in the same breath as the illustrious jobs of anyone else. Stories can help produce that link with the past and also infuse in children a healthy identity for the future.

Stories can link us to our distinctive cultural and spiritual roots. Storyteller and preacher Fred Craddock tells about touring Israel with a guide named Jonah.

> Going from Tel Aviv to Jerusalem, Jonah decided to take us a roundabout way. At one point, he pulled the Volkswagen off to the side of the road and said, "I want to show you something. See that hill over there?" We nodded. "See those trees?" Yeah.
>
> "You can't see it, but there's a road over there. During the war, they thought we were going to come down that road. So they got up in the trees and were going to ambush us. But we heard about it. We came around the other way over the top of that hill, and we killed every one of the would-be ambushers."
>
> I asked Jonah, "Was that in the war of 1948 or 1967?"
>
> He said, "It was the Maccabean War."
>
> I was amazed at the way he told a story that was 2,000 years old. I said, "You tell that story like you were there."
>
> With a level gaze he said to me, "I was."

Reflecting on this experience, Craddock made an observation about his fellow church members: "I don't hear many of our church folks saying, 'We were in the catacombs,' 'We were in Bethlehem' or 'We were in Nazareth.'...Anybody who can't remember any further back than his or her own birth is an orphan."

Stories have the power to turn orphans into full-fledged members of the family.

Stories Help Adults and Children Communicate

Stories are a prime medium for communicating with children—not just talking to children, but creating an environment in which children can share their honest feelings with an adult.

One parent, Keith Meyer, finds nightly bedtime stories with his six-year-old son invaluable.

"It guarantees that I have an unhurried conversation with Kyle at least once a day. And that's important. Last week, after I told a story and before we said our bedtime prayers, I asked, 'Well, Kyle, what do you remember that happened today?'

" 'Mom got angry at me and didn't let me finish my lunch,' he said. When I asked what happened, he said his younger sister yanked his soup bowl off the table, spilling it on the floor. He then pushed his sister away, knocking her down. His mother walked in just in time to see the mess and the push, and she banished Kyle to his room. 'But it wasn't my fault, Dad.'

"We were able to talk about it. He needed to explain his side of things, and I explained that he should call his mother instead of pushing. It was a good conversation. And I might have missed it if I hadn't taken the time to be with him.

"Kids don't open up on demand. If I'd rushed in and asked, 'What happened today?' he'd have said, 'Nothing.' That's all you'll get if that's all the time you spend. Getting kids to be open with you takes time. Our bedtime stories and prayers provide that time."

That father's storytelling has paid off in a better relationship with his son. This leads to a related benefit: *Stories are a way to learn the language your children understand.*

Children are not always able to express themselves verbally. Nor are they always able to understand adults when adults talk to them. For children, play is their language, an expression of their inner world.

In his book *Play Therapy,* child psychologist Garry Landreth writes, "Children's problems are often compounded by the inability of adults in their lives to understand or to respond effectively to what children are feeling or attempting to communicate. Play is to the child what verbalization is to the adult. It is the medium for expressing feelings, exploring relationships, describing experiences, and disclosing wishes and self-fulfillment.... Adults communicate more effectively than through language by their participation in the child's play."

If play is the language of kids, it's important to speak their language by wrestling on the floor, getting your fingers into the Play-Doh, learning a video game. Stories are another way to play, to enter their world and speak a language much different from the language of instruction, explanation and correction.

Joanne Thompson, a parent in Wheat Ridge, Colorado, said, "Our twelve-year-old is quiet, disciplined and reflective. She loves to cook, and she loves books. When my husband, Roger, tucks her in at bedtime, she will often say, 'Dad, tell me a story about when you were a little boy.'

"Roger retrieves past memories and, for a few brief moments, his fatigue is transfigured into the carefree world of a child—scooters, chocolate-covered cherries, the clay pits and Christmas morning. In the glow of the night-light, Jill participates in her father's life."

It's not instruction. It's a shared moment of play for a dad and daughter—a moment that communicates more than any lecture.

Stories Help Children Develop Skills

A number of developmental skills are enhanced by stories. Through stories, children learn vocabulary, creative problem solving and linear thinking. They learn cause/effect relationships. They develop imagination.

One of the wonderful stages of a child's development is when he or she begins to make connections—to see how one aspect of life compares or contrasts with another.

When our daughter Stacey was four, we gave her a small

toy elephant mounted on a plastic base, with an internal string holding the legs, body and head in place. Pressing two buttons on either side of the base slackened the string and caused the elephant to collapse.

Stacey enjoyed making the elephant's legs wobble. "Look, Daddy," she said. "This elephant is just like Bambi!"

Weeks earlier, we had read the story of Bambi. Together we had laughed as the little fawn walked onto a frozen pond and his legs slipped out from under him. I realized the power of stories when, more than a month later, Stacey connected that incident with a wobbly-legged plastic toy.

I want to encourage making observations, synthesizing, recalling past stories. It is part of developing thinking skills. Such skills are enhanced by exposing children to a wide variety of stories.

Stories Help Build Character

In stories, we meet characters who are brave, kind, ingenious. Through their actions, children can better understand what it means to be loyal, courageous, faithful and just.

Even the whimsical stories of Dr. Seuss present children with valuable role models. Consider, for example, *Horton Hatches the Egg*.

Horton is an elephant who was asked by an irresponsible bird to sit in his nest and keep his egg warm. Horton faithfully guards the egg even though he is ridiculed by other animals. Even though he's captured and sent to a circus, he still sits on the egg.

In the end, the bird finds Horton and, now that the sitting is almost done, demands the egg back. But then the egg hatches—and it's an *elephant*—bird. Dr. Seuss writes: "And it should be, it *should* be, it SHOULD be like that! Because Horton was faithful! He sat and he sat!"

I remember thinking, at age six: *Yes, that's the way it*

should be. Dr. Seuss had communicated something about faithfulness and fairness that no lecture could have accomplished.

Horton Hears a Who is about the same faithful elephant who hears a tiny voice on a flower. Even though he can't see the creature whose voice he heard, Horton goes to great lengths to protect whatever-it-is that's on there. It's a wonderful allegory about how the tiny voice of even the most underprivileged can make a difference. It's about speaking up for one's rights. Without writing a didactic editorial, Dr. Seuss effectively instills in children a sense of justice.

Stories Can Inspire to Greatness

People can be coerced into certain minimum standards of behavior. Laws, for example, can discourage theft. But no law can produce a hero. People cannot be forced to do great things.

As Reinhold Niebuhr once said, "The highest moral and spiritual achievements depend not upon a push but a pull. People must be charmed into [greatness]." Along with personal example, stories are one of the best ways of inspiring a person to virtue, heroism and goodness.

This point is made particularly clear by a story told by Fred Craddock. Craddock was a divinity-school professor who trained preachers. But his outlook on his profession changed one day thanks to a story.

> My wife and I used to vacation in the Smoky Mountains. We loved to stop and eat at a place called the Blackberry Inn. One side of this restaurant was solid glass. You could look out while you were eating and see the mountains. We were there one evening, relaxing, when an old man came to our table.
>
> "You on vacation?" he asked.
>
> "Yes, sir."
>
> "Having a good time?"
>
> I was beginning to think, *Well, we were*. But I said, "Yes, sir."

He said, "Well, I hope you have a good time. What do you do?"

That's none of your business, I thought. *We're on vacation.* I said, "I teach in a seminary."

"Oh, are you a preacher?"

"Well, yes."

He pulled up a chair and said, "I want to tell you a story."

"Well, uh, have a seat here at our table."

He said, "I was born in these mountains. My mother was not married, and in those days that brought great shame. And when we went to town, the other women looked at her and looked at me and began to guess who I was and who my father might be. The reproach that was hers fell upon me, and it was painful. At school the children had a name for me. I hid in the weeds at recess. I ate my lunch alone.

"I started going to a little church back in the hills," he continued. "There was a preacher—a cranky, rough preacher with a bushy, black beard and a booming voice. He scared me but fascinated me. I would go just for the sermon, afraid somebody would speak to me in the earlier part of the service and say, 'What's a boy like you doing in church?' So I would arrive late and leave quickly.

"One Sunday, some of the people queued up in the aisle right after the sermon, and I couldn't get by. I began to chill for fear somebody would say something to me. I tried to get out of there.

"Then I felt a hand on my shoulder. I looked out of the corner of my eye and there was the preacher. I saw his beard, I saw that face, and I thought, *Oh no!*

"That preacher looked at me and said, 'Boy, you're a child of...' He paused and I thought, *Uh oh. He knows.* He said, 'Boy, you're a child of...a child of God. I see a striking resemblance.' Then he swatted me on the bottom and said, 'Go claim your inheritance!' "

I asked the old man, "What's your name?"

"Ben Hooper," he said.

Ben Hooper? I remembered my father telling about the people of Tennessee twice electing an illegitimate governor named Ben Hooper.

Ben looked through the restaurant's glass windows, but he wasn't seeing the mountains. I knew he was seeing the bearded face of a rough, country preacher.

"I was born that day," he said.

17

Old Ben Hooper had simply told a story. But with that one story, he gave Fred Craddock a precious gift. He opened the eyes of this preacher to the possibilities of his profession, to the great power for good that he could use for others.

"Well, it's just a story." Some people think storytelling has about as much chance of changing the world as you have of cracking a concrete wall by throwing egg shells at it.

Now you can believe that if you want to, but I've seen those egg shells hit concrete walls. Strangely enough, it was the walls that shattered.

What Stories Should I Tell?

Everyone likes to hear good stories, but few people enjoy telling them. Why?

Two main reasons are: "I don't know what stories to tell" and "I'm terrible at telling stories." This chapter and the next address these apprehensions and help overcome them.

The warehouse of stories holds an unlimited supply. Yet when we're face to face with a child, sometimes our minds suddenly feel empty. When that happens, we can ask ourselves some of the following questions. They are guaranteed to restock our minds with ideas for enjoyable stories.

What stage of life is my child in?

Some story ideas emerge from thinking about what children can understand. Infants, for instance, cannot understand the meanings of words, but that doesn't mean they won't enjoy a story. For infants, a story means the warmth of a lap. It means being held close. It means hearing calming, or sometimes funny, sounds.

Most parents are better than they think they are at telling stories to infants. Parents don't realize that even the games they play with infants are actually stories. For instance:

> *This little piggy went to market.* (Grab child's big toe)
> *This little piggy stayed home.* (Grab second toe)
> *This little piggy had roast beef.* (Grab third toe)

This little piggy had none. (Grab fourth toe)
And this little piggy... (Grab smallest toe)
Went wee, wee, wee, all the way home. (Wiggle smallest toe)

The building anticipation as each toe is touched has often produced rapt attention—even from infants. And the story's climax, the "wee, wee, wee," usually delivered in falsetto, has produced many a child's first chuckle.

Or how about:

Forehead bumper, (Lightly touch child's forehead)
Eye blinker, (Touch child's eyelashes)
Nose dripper, (Touch child's nose)
Mouth eater, (Touch child's lips)
Chin chopper, (Touch child's chin)
Gully, Gully, Gully! (Tickle child under the chin)

For my daughter Kelsey, this saying was how she learned to make other people laugh. She couldn't say the words, but she would point to her daddy's forehead and eyes—and then mercilessly tickle his throat. She hadn't learned the secret of building suspense, but she knew how to deliver the punch line! She was beginning to understand the idea of a story.

When children are a bit older, they enjoy the cadence of nursery rhymes. This is an important step for children. According to educator and child expert Nancy Larrick, "Few adults seem to realize that a baby's experience with language in the first months and years will strongly affect his or her skill in speaking, listening, reading and writing in school."

This is the time for parents to recall their favorite rhymes from childhood. Chances are, they are just as approriate today as they were back then.

For instance, the following nursery-rhyme riddle is at least one thousand years old and has appeared in eight European languages. It asks: What, when broken, can never be repaired, not even by the strongest or wisest individuals?

Humpty Dumpty sat on a wall.
Humpty Dumpty had a great fall.
All the king's horses
And all the king's men
Couldn't put Humpty Dumpty together again.

Who was Humpty? Thanks to illustrations we've seen over the years, we know the answer: an egg. Even before children recognize this as a riddle or a story, they enjoy the sounds and rhythms of the words.

As children develop more comprehension and ability with words, they are ready for more complex stories. Once children are old enough to understand words, we can ask additional questions to spark story ideas.

What has the child experienced recently?

We all learn from our experiences in life, but children, especially, have problems making sense of events. Stories can help. And a child's experiences, in turn, provide a valuable source for story material.

This four-step process can help turn everyday events into stories:

- Select a recent experience—an accident, a celebration, a failure, a joyous event, a painful event—anything you and the child remember.
- Review the event. What happened? How did you feel? How did the child feel? Were others involved? How would they have felt?
- Reflect on the experience. What was learned? Has anyone been changed as a result? Would it be nice if this happened again? How can those involved benefit from this experience?
- Think of ways that the experience could be retold, with names and details changed, as a story the child would appreciate.

Not long ago, my daughter experienced a common childhood trauma: rejection. Stacey and her friend Michelle argued. Michelle ended the conversation by saying emphatically, "I'm never going to be your friend again. And no one else is ever going to be your friend either!"

Stacey, in tears, ran into the house, certain that she was going to be friendless the rest of her days. I tried to ease the pain. My insistence that Michelle didn't mean what she said rang hollow. Even saying that Michelle was wrong was unconvincing. Stacey felt like an exile.

Two things finally helped: time and a story. I waited until our regular bath-and-bedtime routine. By then, some of the day's pain had subsided. The bedtime story helped put it away completely.

> Once there was a little girl named Sarah who loved to climb fences. She had two friends, Maria and Sean, who also liked to climb fences. When the fences were too slippery, Sarah and Maria and Sean would help each other.
>
> But one day when Sean was gone, Sarah slipped and fell down, right on top of Maria. Maria was angry. "Why don't you watch where you're going?" she said. "You did that on purpose!"
>
> "It was an accident," said Sarah. "Are you okay?" "It was not an accident," shouted Maria. "You hurt my arm on purpose."
>
> "No, I didn't."
>
> "Yes, you did. And I don't like you. You're not my friend anymore," said Maria. "I'm going home and I'm never going to play with you again."
>
> Sarah said, "Wait. I'm still your friend."
>
> "No, you're not. No one will ever be your friend again—not me, not Sean, not anybody." And with that, Maria ran home.
>
> How do you think Sarah felt? Yes, very sad. Very lonely. She didn't think anyone would ever play with her again. She went home and cried until supper.
>
> Suddenly, there was a knock on the door. It was Sean, who asked, "Can Sarah come out and climb fences?"
>
> "I thought you didn't want to be my friend," Sarah said when she met Sean at the door.
>
> "Says who?" said Sean.
>
> "Maria."

"Well, it's not true. Can you come out and climb?"

"Sure, but what if Maria is angry?"

"She won't be," said Sean. "She has a short memory. I don't think she remembers anything she says."

And sure enough, as soon as Sarah and Sean got to the fence, out came Maria, ready to climb.

"Do you remember what you're never going to be?" Sarah asked. But Maria said, "Huh?" and Sarah knew that Sean was right. Just because Maria said something didn't mean it was true.

They had a great time climbing fences.

No, it's not great literature, but it did the job for the preschooler in our house. The next day Stacey and Michelle were happily playing again.

Stories can help interpret life's events and put them into perspective. Whenever a child has gone through a difficult experience, telling a story can be therapeutic. After all, this may be the first time the child has ever experienced a particular emotion; he or she may have no idea how to handle these feelings.

The technique for telling such a story is simple. Another boy or girl (don't choose the name of the child actually involved) goes through a similar experience and yet finds that he or she can get over it and enjoy life again.

What will the child be experiencing in the next few days or weeks?

For another source of story material, think about what the child will be doing in the next few days. Hearing stories can be a great way to prepare for new events.

If the family is going to see a movie, for example, it's often a good idea to tell the story ahead of time. My family did this with the Disney movies *Snow White* and *The Rescuers*. The children enjoyed the movies much more because they already had the basic plot in mind. They were free to enjoy the additional detail the movie added. (Of course, you might

Everyday events can be confusing or frightening when experienced by a child for the first time. Stories can shed light on the unknowns and prepare listeners for the experiences ahead. The difference between fear and fun may be the difference between hearing a story and not hearing one.

The following story starter provides a jumping-off point for telling a story in preparation for a child's often-traumatic first haircut.

First, Brian tripped over rocks. Then, it was bigger things that he bumped into—his sister's bicycle, his mother's cabinet, a stack of books beside his own bed. When he didn't see his new model airplane lying on the floor—and broke it in two with one careless step—he knew he had to do something.

The problem was his hair. It was so long that Brian barely could see anything at all. Realizing that something had to be done as soon as possible, he decided to...

Such a story could go on to detail what Brian will experience when he goes to the barber. In addition, it has made Brian the initiator of the action; rather than being *made to do something,* he decides to do it on his own initiative.

not want to do this with a movie that has a surprise ending, allowing the children to enjoy the surprise. Even so, in most cases children don't seem to mind seeing a surprise scene over and over—even though they know what's coming.)

If your child is going to be attending or participating in a wedding, the weeks preceding are an excellent time to tell stories about weddings you've been to or even a story specifically about the upcoming event.

In a few days, Aunt Karen is going to get married to Uncle Matt, and you're going to help by doing something very important. You'll get all dressed up in white, and they'll give you a basket to carry, and you'll stand in front of a long aisle. Then, when Mr. Bowman tells you to, you'll walk slowly down the aisle until you stand right next to Cousin Pat. What part do you think will be the most fun? Right—cakes and mints afterward!

Even less momentous events can be the occasion for a story. I call them "bedtime briefings." For instance, on Saturday night, as I'm tucking the girls in, I tell them about the good things to expect at church the next day—the friends they're going to see, the things they're going to do. I also try to tell them what to listen for; I give them a foretaste of any lesson or sermon they'll be hearing. If I know the Sunday school lesson (and most teachers are eager to tell you so you can prepare their students), I'll tell the Bible story. My girls then feel more confident when they hear the story the next day. They also appreciate the background details I'm able to supply—information that often has to be left out of time-constrained Sunday school lessons.

For instance, once the teacher was telling the story of Jesus healing a blind man. My three-year-old daughter was eager to tell the class, "The blind man's name was Bartimaeus," a detail the teacher had overlooked. The next week, when the lesson was about Noah's ark, my daughter was troubled because she knew the names of Noah's sons—Ham, Shem and Japheth—but I couldn't supply the names of their wives. Her inquiring mind wanted to know!

Besides building confidence, stories can also comfort children who are fearful of the unknown. Stories can tell them what to expect; they can assure children that things will turn out all right.

A few years ago, while camping, our daughter dislocated her elbow. On the way to the hospital, I realized I could say "It will be okay" only so many times before the words ceased to be meaningful.

Despite her discomfort, Stacey was calmed by stories of "when Daddy was a boy and got whacked with a bat and had to go to the emergency room." Then her mother told a story about "when I was girl and fell off a horse and broke my arm and had to go to the doctor." Stacey wanted to know what the doctors would do, and the stories of doctors helping Mom and Dad—and everything turning out okay—calmed everyone down as we drove to the hospital.

At the emergency room, Stacey willingly let the doctor examine her arm, even though it continued to hurt. She knew that the doctor would help her arm get better. How did she know? A story told her so.

Where are we?

Another source of story ideas is your immediate environment. Stories always have more impact if the surroundings reinforce the mood or provide some visual atmosphere for the story. Here are some of the typical settings that can be used for storytelling.

One of the advantages storytelling has over reading books to your children is that you can be doing something else at the same time—such as driving. On extended trips, particularly, the towns and countryside you're driving through can be the story starter.

When we were driving to visit relatives in Tennessee, I pointed to the forests along the road and asked about the most famous Tennessean I could think of. "Did I ever tell you the story of Davy Crockett, who lived in Tennessee hills just like those over there?"

The next several miles were taken up with stories, legends and tall tales about the famous frontiersman, how he "lived in the woods and he knew every tree, and killed him a bear when he was only three." I told the famous yarn about how Davy once encountered a grizzly bear and, not wanting to fight the ferocious beast, managed to "grin it down" and go on his way. Afterward, the hills and forests along the road seemed more interesting to everyone in the car.

The stories sparked by what you see through the windshield don't have to be limited to historically based docudrama, however. While driving through Wisconsin, we again tried to think of the most famous thing about the state— dairy products—and the following story emerged.

Once there was a little mouse who was afraid of cheese. And for a mouse, that's a terrible condition. Mommy Mouse tried everything she could think of—putting cheese in a sandwich, covering it with ketchup, even cutting it up into tiny pieces. But the little mouse was still too afraid. He wouldn't even touch cheese.

His mommy tried something different. One day after the little mouse had been playing outside, he came in for supper. Mommy Mouse said, "Tonight we'll get you to stop being afraid of cheese."

"But how?" asked the little mouse.

"Sit here," said Mommy, pointing to a chair at the table. The little mouse looked at the plate in front of him and saw three kinds of cheese—Cheddar, Swiss and Muenster.

"But I'm afraid of cheese!" said the little mouse.

"Don't worry," said his mother. "You don't have to eat it. You don't have to touch it. I just want you to look at it and make sure no one else eats it. Can you do that without being afraid?"

"Yes."

So that's what the little mouse did. He watched and watched. And after a while he began to feel hungry. He looked at the cheese. He still didn't want to touch it, but it was beginning to look less threatening.

Finally he picked up just a tiny bit of Cheddar cheese. He was touching it, and it didn't seem dangerous. Then his stomach gurgled, and he remembered how hungry he was. He put just a tiny piece of the cheese into his mouth.

He was surprised! It tasted good!

Before he knew what was happening, he had eaten all the cheese on his plate and had asked his mother for some more. He knew he wouldn't be frightened of cheese ever again.

That story led into an interesting discussion in the car about the kinds of things *we* are scared of. The miles quickly rolled by.

The possibilities are endless. Wherever you are, ask yourself, "What do I associate with this area?" If you're in Norway, for instance, you might think of trolls; create a story about those strange, malformed creatures. If on a ship, you might think of explorers; tell stories of Columbus, Leif Erikson or Magellan—all of whom sailed off for places unknown, having no idea what they'd see.

If you cross a bridge, you might tell the story of "The Three Billy Goats Gruff" who also had to cross a bridge and overcome the mean (and hungry!) troll who lived beneath it.

At the dinner table, it's amazing how many stories come to mind about a character who faces dangerous situations and needs strength—and finds it by eating a particular vegetable that, coincidentally, we just happen to be serving that night.

The story of Popeye the sailor rescuing his friend Olive Oyl from the evil clutches of Bluto, after gulping down several bites of spinach, has stood the test of time. But peas, potatoes, beans and carrots have been the source of superhuman energy, power and quickness for countless other heroes in our dinner-time stories.

During bath time, other stories might be suggested by the setting. The story of Jonah and the big fish, for instance, or Noah and his homemade ark. Or you can make up something specifically about children and baths. For instance:

> Once there was a girl who never took a bath. She went outside and played hard and got herself very dirty, but she wouldn't let anyone wash her. Day after day, she got more and more dirt on her hands and face. One morning she woke up and looked in the mirror.
>
> There, growing in the dirt behind her left ear, was a bright yellow dandelion! She tried to pull it out, but the roots were too deep. She didn't know what she would do. Her father said, "Maybe I should get a lawn mower and cut it off." The little girl didn't think that was a good idea.
>
> She tried to think of other ways to get it off. [You can come up with any number of outrageous possibilities.] Nothing worked. She was getting tired of the flower because it attracted bees, and she didn't like their buzzing.
>
> Finally, she said, "I guess I have to water this flower, don't I?" So she climbed into the bathtub and rubbed a wet washcloth behind her ear. Then, to her great surprise and relief, the dandelion and all the dirt came off. After that, the little girl took a bath every night that she was dirty.

Bedtime, of course, is the traditional time for a story. Many parents have learned that a bedtime ritual doesn't guarantee a child will go to sleep, but it can create an atmosphere conducive to restfulness. It can be a special time of enjoyment and interaction between adult and child. The security of knowing everything is okay—with parents and with the characters in the stories—will help children relax.

At bedtime, perhaps you think of stories of famous sleepers—Sleeping Beauty, Rip Van Winkle, "The Princess and the Pea," or a story about a child who went to sleep and awoke to have an exciting adventure. The only caution I'd offer is that the stories should probably come to a peaceful and happy ending. Otherwise, you may have a sleepless child to cope with for several more hours!

I've also taken advantage of the bedtime setting—and the children's blankets—to tell stories about people who live in tents. As we huddle under the covers, a story about desert nomads or tepee dwellers or backpackers seems to take on more immediacy.

When telling stories, the storyteller can decide exactly how long the story should be. Unlike reading a book, there are no requisite pages to turn. (And children can be very observant, detecting and preventing any attempt to abbreviate the reading of a favorite book.) When stories come to a reasonable ending, they can satisfy the child's need for resolution and the adult's need for a timely conclusion.

What stories do I enjoy?

Perhaps the most important element in good storytelling is finding the right story for you. Some of us, due to our particular personalities, naturally enjoy adventure stories.

> Stephen and Sylvia found themselves captured by pirates and tied up in a cave surrounded by treasure. The only way out was for Sylvia to pick up a jeweled dagger in her teeth, cut the ropes and...

Others naturally think of humorous, slapstick or absurd situations.

> Amanda was walking through the garden, when suddenly a large tomato leaped from a nearby vine, landing with a sploosh right on her new shoes. As she looked around, she realized more tomatoes were grinning at her, ready to jump. What was causing them to play "Splatter the Shoes"? Well, of course, it was the coming of the Summer Sillies, the urge everyone has, when it gets hot, to do crazy things. Amanda felt it herself. In fact, she was about ready to...

Still others prefer romance, history, intrigue or animal stories. What is your taste in literature? At least at the beginning, you'll probably want to choose stories that suit your tastes. Before long, you'll branch out into other types, especially as you discover the interests of the children to whom you're telling stories. But in the beginning, tell the stories that you most enjoy. Those will be the stories you'll tell with the most relish—and your young listeners will enjoy your enjoyment along with the story itself.

How to Tell a Good Story

Do you recognize the name Scheherazade? She was the harem princess whose sultan selected one woman for each night and then, in the morning, executed the unfortunate woman.

When Scheherazade was chosen, she wasn't ready to accept this sitruation. At the end of her one-night stand, she told the sultan a fascinating story, ending her tantalizing tale with a "to be continued." Even though the sultan wanted to get on with the morning-after execution, he couldn't kill her. He had to know how the story ended.

She did the same thing the next night, and the next, and the next. As author and speaker Calvin Miller observes, "For once in history, story conquered *eros,* and Scheherazade lived to tell the story, or rather a thousand stories." The sheik kept her. The result was *Arabian Nights,* compliments of Scheherazade, a highly motivated storyteller.

Not everyone has Scheherazade's need to succeed as a spellbinder, but each of us is a potential storyteller. We can all relate our own experiences with enthusiasm, conviction and an abundance of detail. Why? Because we're interested in what we've experienced, we have seen it happen and we want to tell others about it. These are the essentials of good storytelling: identifying with what we tell, seeing a mental picture of the events and having a desire to share the story. Yet many potential storytellers never take the first step, afraid their listeners will tune them out or, worse, yawn with boredom.

Storytelling is an art that can be learned. Reluctant storytellers can build confidence by mastering only a few basic skills. It's amazing how frustration about storytelling can change after one learns a few key principles. And when we know what to do, we'll find more opportunities to put our newfound talents to good use.

The Place to Start

Instead of getting bogged down in a study of storytelling techniques, the best way to learn is to tell stories to an audience that doesn't know a good story from a bad one! The easiest way to do that is to start with two- or three-year-olds—an age group that isn't likely to embarrass you, no matter what you say. Even if you quit in mid-sentence and say, "Well, that's all I can think of. Wasn't that an interesting story?" in most cases, your audience will be delighted just to have an adult spend time with them.

Try very short stories at first. Don't try to go any longer than you or the child can remain interested. After all, the object is not to complete an epic but to enjoy a story and spark the imagination.

I would suggest making up stories for this group. Create them as you go along. Start telling a story even if you don't know how it will end. Under the pressure of finding an ending to that story, you'll create some very good stuff. Don't worry if it isn't of literary quality. Getting started in storytelling—even with some clinkers—is much better than never starting at all.

Here are some opening lines. Feel free to take them any direction you'd like to go.

> Once there was a raccoon who never washed his hands before he ate. All the other raccoons would wash their hands, even their food before they ate, but not Ricky...

Have you ever seen a boy who could jump higher than a tree? Not many people have. But Marcus could. And all the other boys...

One day Frieda and Felix woke up, and their room was filled with bubbles. Where did they come from? They decided to find out. But first—how to find the door?

Have you ever heard the story of the hunter who went hunting with crooked arrows? All of his arrows were crooked, and when he shot them they...

I've started these stories without knowing how they would end. But with a set of young eyes staring at me, the pressure of having to bring them to some sort of conclusion brought some things to mind.

Often the hardest part of storytelling is the act of getting started. The following additional opening lines will help spark ideas and get the storytelling ball rolling. In time, the most difficult part of storytelling might be finding the time to finish all the interesting stories you've begun!

Penny looked up at the grey sky and wished it would rain something fun—like marshmallows—instead of cold, wet raindrops. Suddenly she felt a soft plop on the top of her head. Looking up, she couldn't believe her eyes! It was...

Paul had never visited a museum before, so he didn't really know what to expect. That's why he wasn't too surprised when one of the statues leaned over and whispered...

Everyone else said Mrs. Lawrence was a spy. But when the Thomas twins peeked through her basement window, they were amazed to see she was really...

As much as she liked her little brother, Sara Snail occasionally wanted to be all alone. Yet, somehow her brother was able to find her—no matter how hard she tried to hide. Then, one day, she...

Long, long ago lived a tyrannosaurus named Tim, who only liked things that began with the letter t: teacups, tennis shoes, traffic lights and tap dancing, for example. But there was one "t" thing that Tim couldn't stand...

Pamela didn't believe in the Mushroom People until, one day, she looked at the ground and noticed a mushroom with a small front door in its stem. Curious, she bent down and pressed the tiny doorbell...

For instance, with Frieda and Felix and the bubbles, Felix decided to climb out the window and get away, forgetting that he was in an upstairs room. He fell and hurt his leg. When Frieda heard his cry, she started crawling through the bubbles to find out where they were coming from. She discovered they were coming out of the drain in the bathtub! So she put in the plug, and with the source cut off, the bubbles soon popped and disappeared. Then Frieda could run outside and help Felix get a bandage for his scraped leg.

There's nothing particularly clever about the story—no hidden symbolism or social commentary. It's just a way to resolve the situation created in the opening line. Other people will, no doubt, develop the idea much differently. That's fine. What was important was that two preschoolers enjoyed listening to a story—and Dad became more comfortable telling them one.

With older children, sometimes the best way to begin is by telling true stories about the events of the day. Not only does it build relationships within the group, but it also helps create an atmosphere conducive to stories.

An acquaintance of mine says that in his family everyone gets involved in storytelling. His contention is that everyone has a story to tell—he or she just may not know it. People simply need the right opportunity to trigger it.

"We have a custom. Whenever the family is together for a meal," he says, "we ask a question that everyone has to answer. Most often we ask, 'What was the worst thing that happened to you today?' Everybody has to tell something. Laura always says the same thing: 'The school bell rang at 8:30.' And when we get around to 'What was the best thing that happened today?' Laura always says, 'It rang again at 3:30.' And out of that family experience, we all learned how to tell stories."

Other questions to ask include:

- Who is the person you most want to be like? Who is one person you don't want to be like? Why?

- When do you remember being the most happy? the most sad?
- If you had a whole week during which you could do anything you wanted, what would you do?
- If you could spend a day with anyone (not including the people in this room) who would it be? What would you do?

A variation is to sit in a circle and guess how the person to your left would answer the question. After you guess, have that person give the real answer. This way, you'll likely double the number of story possibilities.

Whatever your approach, these questions spark ideas that can be expressed with a short, descriptive story. Most people find the thinking enjoyable. With a set or two of attentive ears to listen, it is the perfect atmosphere for non-storytellers to begin to tell stories.

Techniques of Good Storytelling

After you've told a few stories, you'll start thinking about ways to make them even more enjoyable and entertaining for your listeners. Most of us want to transform our audience from voluntary listeners (who decide, out of politeness or obligation, to listen) to involuntary listeners who can't help but listen, who are so intrigued by the story that they can't pull themselves away.

Here are a few simple steps that can help you tell stories that will capture a child's rapt attention.

Setting Them Up

Some people believe that to capture the interest of children stories have to start with a chase scene or someone dangling off a bridge. I haven't found that necessary. Children like to get on the bus and get settled before you go roaring off. Creating the right opening atmosphere is crucial.

You can't just walk up to a storyteller and say, "Hey, I hear you tell good stories. Tell me one." That would be like confronting a comedian by saying, "I hear you're funny. Okay, say something to make me laugh." It doesn't work like that. A story, like humor, depends on its context.

Most storytellers take the time to build the occasion before they tell a story. Even the best tale is ruined if the listeners are unable or unready to give their attention. Good storytellers make sure their listeners are prepared.

If you're with a group of children, you can say, "Would all of you who like to laugh raise your hands." This suggests that the story will be funny, and you have set a mood that will elicit giggles and laughter in response to whatever you tell. On the other hand, if you want to create an atmosphere of suspense or adventure, turn down the lights or light a candle. You also can start the story at a slower tempo.

I've heard of one father who would come home at night, go to the sink, wash his hands, and say something like, "I hope I never again see what I saw today." That's all he would say. One of his children would eventually ask, "Well, Daddy, what did you see today?" He'd say, "Oh, are you kids here? I thought that was your mother. Never mind."

Their curiosity up, the kids would have to know. "What was it, Dad?"

"I don't know if this is anything for kids."

"You can just tell us part of it. What was it?"

"Well, I suppose so." And after what seemed like an eternity, he'd slowly unravel a tall tale, loosely based on his experiences of the day, to a fully prepared audience.

Other storytellers use props to set up their listeners. You can turn a small table upside down and ask the child to pretend it's a boat—"Did I ever tell you about the fisherman who caught a fish that had a coin in its mouth?"—or whatever boat story you can think of.

Even in telling bedtime stories, you can set the scene. One father said, "When our children were small, I would make up stories to tell them at night. But I found I had to prepare —touch the child, fix the covers, ask 'Are you comfortable?'

and 'What did you enjoy doing today?' Finally I would get around to 'Did I ever tell you about the time when I was your age?' "

That father prepared the context for his story. Storyteller Fred Craddock puts it this way:

"Picture an old man peeling an apple for his grandson. Grandpa pulls out an old Barlow knife that he uses for everything, opens it up, rubs it on his breeches—after all it's his grandson and he doesn't want any germs—and he starts peeling. Real slow. Gradually the curl lengthens, hanging almost to the floor, and Grandpa says, 'You know, one time I peeled thirty-five of these before I ever broke a peel.'

"Now what's happening to the kid? The juices are flowing. The stomach is saying, 'I thought I was going to get an apple.' The mouth is watering. The kid is ready to eat! But Grandpa just keeps going. Finally the peel drops at his feet. The kid lunges for the apple. 'Wait just a minute,' says Grandpa. 'Let me get the core out for you.' It seems as if it takes him forever. But when the kid finally tastes the apple, it is the best apple in the world.

"Now contrast that with walking up to a vending machine, putting in a couple of quarters, pushing a button, grabbing an apple, and eating it as you hurry off to someplace else. The stomach is saying, 'I didn't ask for that!'

"I think of those scenes whenever I start to tell a story. I want to prepare the ears to hear."

Adding Excitement

If you've readied the children for the story, you now have little eyes looking at you and little ears waiting to hear. Several tools are available to keep the attention you've gotten.

Your own interest. Focused enthusiasm is usually contagious with children. If you're excited about something, they'll want to check it out. If you find something interesting in a children's story, your listeners are much more likely to be intrigued by it, too. Don't disguise your own enjoyment of the story—tell it as though you really love it, consider it important and want to share it.

Facial expressions. Raised eyebrows, grimaces, frowns, eyes wide with fear—all these can be used effectively to communicate the mood of the story and to maintain the attention of your listeners. It's possible, of course, to overdramatize and thus turn off your audience. Whatever the emotion, find an appropriate way to express it nonverbally as well as verbally. You'll know you're communicating well when you see your expressions mirrored in the children's faces. You'll know you've overdone it if they turn their faces toward one another and cut up.

Vocal inflections. Varying your voice can also keep your listeners with you. You can excite them with a louder voice. You can calm them with a soft, low voice. Often a whisper is more effective than a shout for communicating a very important line.

You can suggest different voices for different characters in your stories, but you don't need to be an impersonator. In fact, overdoing the characterizations can distract children from the story itself. It's best to keep the story conversational, simple and direct. It's just as effective to say, "And the girl with the squeaky voice said..." as it is to try to provide the squeaky voice yourself. Unless you're simply wanting to be silly, and the children are enjoying the silliness, usually only one character per story should ever have a distinctive manner of speaking.

Tempo. Any signs of weariness or indifference among your listeners indicate you should change your pacing. Usually it means you should quicken the tempo; although, if you've been rushing along for several minutes, you can regain interest by pausing and saying, "But then, something very strange and different happened." Then slowly, building suspense, describe the mysterious transformation that befell one of the characters.

If changing the pace doesn't work, perhaps you can skip over some details that, in the telling, would bore your listeners. Instead of forcing an unwanted story, it's better to move quickly to an ending or even to say, "Well, I don't think this story is quite what we want today. Let's save it for another time."

Eye contact. As a rule, it's better to look directly at the children to whom you are telling the story. This benefits both listener and teller.

For listeners, the story comes through with greater immediacy when the storyteller maintains direct eye contact. It helps each child feel as if you are speaking personally. Eyes can also communicate the mood of the story in ways words cannot, signifying wonder, fear, joy, bewilderment and a host of other emotions.

Eye contact also benefits the teller. We can tell if our listeners are understanding us, and we can experience one of storytelling's greatest joys: seeing the faces of children entranced by the story we're telling. We see them flinch when the main character is surprised; we see their furrowed brows when they fear something bad is going to happen; we see their expressions relax when the main character escapes danger. Enjoy!

At times, you won't be able to use eye contact as you tell stories—when you're driving a car, for instance. Or when you're sitting next to the child's bed in a darkened room telling a bedtime story. At these times, capitalize on the atmosphere you do have—the sights outside the windshield or the mood created by the darkness.

Lighting the Mind's Eye

Good storytellers think visually. Our job is to light up the mind's eye of the listener.

I've found it easier to make up stories by imagining a situation and simply describing what I see. My task is to transfer the images in my mind into images that the children can see in their minds. Doing that involves keeping several concerns in mind.

Inform the imagination. Children often need help visualizing a story. While children can be stimulated to use their imaginations, sometimes their imaginations need to be taught. Children can easily "see" such fantastic creatures as fairies, elves, giants and monsters; even princes and princesses can be imagined much more romantically by children than by adults. Children, though, cannot be expected to come up with even approximations of a real person, animal or place they've never seen.

Before telling children stories about rabbits, foxes, beavers or bears, it's a good idea to make sure they know what such creatures look like. Show the children pictures. Using these visual aids beforehand will help paint a mental picture when the story is told.

Use visual words. A few specific details are sufficient to set the scene and make the story memorable. When Jesus, a master storyteller, told the story of the prodigal son, he didn't describe the boy's emotional condition in psychological terms—he talked about his hunger in terms of his willingness to eat pig feed, his desperation in terms of his willingness to return to his father's house as a servant instead of a son. When Jesus described the celebration at home when the wayward son returns, he mentioned a ring, a robe and a fatted calf.

Nouns and verbs work best. Words like *stadium, referee, cheers* and *goal* immediately put you among the crowd at a football game. Too many adjectives, on the other hand, clutter up the description. It's better to say, "The hawk flew in slow circles over the family of rabbits, who tripped over each other in fright as they raced for the safety of their underground home," rather than, "The big, mean, hungry hawk was flying in the blue, cloudless sky and looking down at the poor, scared rabbits." Adjectives bog down the story and reduce visual excitement. A hawk circling a family of rabbits can be pictured more readily than a "big, mean, hungry hawk."

Use unexpected images. People's minds are like galleries of stored pictures: one vivid scene can establish an opinion that cannot be dislodged by other facts. This is often how prejudices and misinformation stay in the brain.

After a story about a predatory hawk and some scared rabbits, for instance, a child might think of hawks as bad creatures. So later I'll follow up that story with a story about a hawk that saves a field mouse from a snake. Then the child begins to see that hawks, like most creatures (especially people), can be either good or bad, depending on the individual. I'll tell about good grownups and bad grownups, good kids and bad kids, good explorers and bad explorers, good teachers and bad teachers.

When unhealthy attitudes develop, often stories can help correct them. Grudges, for example, are often rooted in pictures. Once our daughter Stacey had been teased and shoved by a classmate. Every time Meghan's name came up in conversation, Stacey would say, "She's mean. She pushed me."

Not wanting one unfortunate incident to cloud Stacey's overall attitude toward Meghan, I started telling stories about three little cats: Stacey Cat, Meghan Cat and Ryan Cat (Ryan was a much-liked friend). The three little cats had all kinds of adventures—climbing trees, hiding from dogs, getting lost—but, in each story, all three cats had to work together to get back home safely.

It wasn't long before Stacey was talking about her *two* best friends: Ryan and Meghan!

Think in terms of changing scenes. When structuring a story, I don't have a mental outline or a list of points to make. Instead, I envision myself as a playwright or screenwriter. I mentally ask myself three questions.

- Where are we? (and describe the location)
- Who's there? (and identify the characters present)

- What's happening? (and report the actions and conversations)

Changing any of the variables can change the scene. Maybe the location changes. Or maybe a new character enters. Or maybe the characters and location are constant, but something unexpected happens. The plot of the story, then, is simply telling what happens in one scene, and then changing the scene.

Using this approach, we can "see" what's happening. When we describe what we're "seeing," our listeners' imaginations are stirred, and our stories have movement. They are more visual and, as a result, our listeners will see, feel and enjoy the story to a greater degree.

Using Dialogue

Consider these two lines: "The master told the servant that he had done a good job" and "The master said, 'Well done, good and faithful servant.'" Which has more impact? Most of us would say the second sentence. Why? Because we hear the actual words the master used. Showing is always preferable to telling. And by using direct quotations, we show our listeners what's being said; we don't just tell them.

In storytelling, direct quotations are almost always better than indirect quotations. Instead of saying, "The girl told her friends that because of their disagreements, she was leaving," it's more arresting to say, "The girl told her friends, 'I'm tired of arguing with you. I'm going away, and I'm not coming back!'"

Actual quotes create the sense that we're overhearing the conversation. Listeners will involve themselves by imagining what the characters looked like when they said those words.

Beware Rhetorical Questions

Children naturally assume that if storytellers ask a question, they want an answer. They don't understand questions that do not call for a response.

One storyteller, in the midst of a story about cats, made the mistake of asking rhetorically, "One morning the boy looked in the garden, and what do you think he saw?"

"An elephant," one child said quickly and confidently.

"No, dear," said the storyteller. "It was just a *small* garden."

"It was a small elephant," the child firmly replied.

The story about cats was ruined. The kitten that the storyteller had hoped to introduce was now an anticlimax. Finding an elephant in the garden is a much more interesting idea than finding a kitten. The options are either to try making up a story about a garden-variety elephant or to say something like "The elephant was in a different garden. In this garden, the boy saw a curious sight: a kitten that had not been there the night before."

In either case, the lesson to learn is not to ask questions unless you want an answer—and are prepared to incorporate it into the story.

Repetition Is Not, Is Not a Bad Word

One of the marks of children's stories that some would-be storytellers overlook is the importance of repetition. Whatever else may be abbreviated when condensing stories, repetitive phrases should be retained because of the appeal they have for the child and the invitation to participate that they offer.

How much shorter—and tamer—would "The Gingerbread Man" be without the refrain, "Run, run, run, as fast as you can; you can't catch me, I'm the Gingerbread Man." Many children can't resist joining in with gusto.

Likewise with "The Three Little Pigs." Much of its appeal is in the Big Bad Wolf's dread greeting, "Little pig, little pig, let me come in," the pig's rejoinder, "Not by the hairs on my chinny-chin-chin," and the wolf's threat, "Then I'll huff, and I'll puff, and I'll bloooow your house down," repeated for each of the three pigs.

It is the same with the story of Henny Penny, who is sure the sky is falling. Much of the story's popularity is no doubt due to the repetition of the names of her companions: Cocky-locky, Ducky-wucky, Goosey-loosey, Turkey-lurkey and the villainous Foxy-woxy.

Three Simple Keys

Storyteller John Masefield identifies three key elements of his craft: "Remarkable openings, proper pauses and notable climaxes."

Certainly other elements contribute to good storytelling. But to conclude our consideration of the fundamentals of good storytelling technique, let's look at the three important items Masefield mentions.

Openings. The first two or three sentences of a story should do three things: establish the setting, introduce the main characters and give some indication of what the story will be about.

For instance, "Once upon a time, a poor widow lived with her only son, Jack, and a cow named Milky-white, and she was their only fortune." This standard fairy-tale opening establishes the magical, faraway nontime and place; introduces Jack; and suggests that the family's meager resources will be a significant factor in the development of the tale.

Some opening lines fail to do this. Consider this one from Walter de la Mare's "The Three Sleeping Boys of Warwickshire": "In a low-ceilinged, white-washed room on the uppermost floor of a red-brick building in Pleasant Street, Cheriton, standing there in the glazed cases, is a collection of shells, conches, sea-weeds, dried salty flowers, fossils, staring birds, goggling fish with starry eyes..."

Children listening to such an introduction might be excused if they asked, "When are you going to start the story?"

Much better is the beginning of Hans Christian Andersen's "The Tinder Box": "A soldier came marching along the high road, left, right, left, right. He had his knapsack on his back and a sword at his side, for he had been to the wars and was returning home. And on the road he met a Witch—a horrid-looking creature..."

We know right away that the soldier will have to be at his bravest and most resourceful if he is to make it home intact.

Pauses. The dramatic pause is an effective tool best employed immediately before important turning points. Children have quick minds and often can guess what's going to happen; a pause prolongs the suspense and gives everyone a chance to enjoy the pleasure of anticipation.

In one Arthurian story, a thief is stealthily edging around a great bronze bell. If he rings it, Arthur's knights will wake up. Slowly he inches by it, step...by...step. What will happen? Rushing too quickly through that part of the story would rob the story of much of its pleasure.

Once the climax has been reached, however, children quickly lose interest. Then, it's time to bring the story to a close.

Endings. The final sentence of the story is important for determining the lasting impression that remains in the child's mind. It must fit the story, tying up any loose ends. Whether the tale is tragic, comic, romantic or adventurous, listeners should feel satisfied that everything has been resolved—the quest ended, the evil dealt with, the "good" characters facing the future confidently.

Patrick Chalmer's "The Little Pagan Faun" ends on an emphatic note:

> So after hearing the Lady's promise, the little pagan faun trotted off into the woods again, munching his cake, and feeling greatly comforted. At that very moment, the clocks struck twelve. It was Christmas Day!

When the story doesn't have a strong punchline, we can provide a sense of completion simply by tone of voice: "And now you've heard the story of Beebee and the talking worm." Intonation can communicate finality and resolution.

But remember, the story isn't over simply because you've

finished telling it. The moments immediately after the ending are also important. If the story has engaged a child's imagination, you may find yourself answering a series of questions or fielding a variety of comments:

"Where are all the dinosaurs now?"

"How could the giant tell it was the blood of an Englishman?"

"If I ever saw a dragon, I'd chop its tail off!"

Instead of being impatient with these questions and claims, take them as compliments. They are a child's way of saying, "You created an interesting world that I've entered. Now I'm reluctant to leave. Since I've been there, I'd like to think about it some more, and I'd like to tell you what I'm thinking." From a child, that's high praise indeed.

Perhaps the greatest tribute that can be paid a storyteller, however, is the moment of silence that sometimes follows your final sentence. Your listeners have been lost in another world, and it takes them a few moments to return to the present.

Don't spoil their pleasure (and your success) by immediately returning to the mundane. The impression you've left on their minds will be destroyed by an abrupt "Now put your things away, and hurry!" The magic of the moment is irrecoverable.

Chapter 4

Different Stories for Different Ages

Once upon a time, childhood was a period of innocence and carefree play. Children were protected and shielded from certain information. Parents said such things as "Let's talk about that later when the children are asleep" or "That's not a good TV show for kids." It was important to let children experience wonder and security.

In today's world, however, the idea of protecting kids has begun to evaporate. Children now are exposed to many things that earlier generations would have dubbed "For mature audiences only." Apparently childhood innocence is no longer considered a positive thing.

Professor David Elkind, in his book *All Grown Up and No Place to Go*, says that youngsters are exposed to every form of human vice and depravity "under the mistaken assumption that this will somehow inure them to evil and prepare them to live successful, if not virtuous and honorable, lives. This assumption rests on the mistaken belief that a bad experience is the best preparation for a bad experience. In fact, the reverse is true: *a good experience is the best preparation for a bad experience.*"

Parents and other adults who tell stories to children can benefit from understanding this changing atmosphere.

Neil Postman's *The Disappearance of Childhood* shows the difference between the current climate for children and the previous climate. The time between 1850 and 1950, he writes, was "the high-water mark of childhood....Successful attempts were made during these years to get all children into school and out of factories, into their own clothing, their own furniture, their own literature, their own games, their own social world.... Children were classified as qualitatively different from adults."

Today the trend is in the opposite direction. Distinctly children's clothing, children's eating habits, children's games and children's tastes in entertainment are disappearing. Their clothes now have the same designer labels as adults'; their movies have as many special effects. Today's children are more and more "little adults," living lives as fast-paced and fashion-conscious as their parents. Is it any wonder that adolescents are now heavily involved in adult crimes, adult sexual practices and adult diseases?

In the rush to adulthood, the joys of childhood are lost. Stories *appropriate to the age level* can rescue those joys, helping children fully experience and enjoy their childhood. "Appropriate to the age level" is the key phrase. Not all stories are suitable for children. In fact, there are dangers in presenting inappropriate subject matter to children.

In earlier generations, adults made information available to children in stages, in ways they could handle psychologically. "The maintenance of childhood depended on the principles of managed information and sequential learning," writes Postman. The invention of mass media began wresting control of information from the home and school. "It altered the kinds of information children could have access to, its quality and quantity, its sequence, and the circumstances in which it would be experienced."

For example, television has much to offer children—exciting entertainment and educational potential—but it threatens childhood. "Television," according to Postman, "operates virtually around the clock. It requires a continuous supply of novel and interesting information to engage and hold an audience. Thus, television must make use of every existing taboo in the culture." It opens secrets, it makes public what previously had been considered private subject matter. It dilutes and demystifies the concept of shame—in television, there is very little to be ashamed of. Instead, everything is to be broadcast.

This includes the glorifying of sexual practice. British columnist G. K. Chesterton once observed, "All healthy men, ancient and modern, Eastern and Western, know that there is a certain fury in sex that we cannot afford to inflame and that a certain mystery and awe must ever surround it if we are to remain sane." Too early and too flippant an exposure to sex can affect a child's attitudes for years to come.

Other taboos appear in stories that glorify self-centeredness, cruelty, greed or materialism. "Civilization cannot exist without the control of impulses, particularly the impulse toward aggression and immediate gratification," writes Postman. "We are in constant danger of being possessed by barbarism, of being overrun by violence, promiscuity, instinct, egoism.... Certainly since the Middle Ages, it has been commonly believed that the impulse toward violence, sexuality and egoism is of particular danger to children, who, it is assumed, are not yet sufficiently governed by self-restraint."

Without a prior orientation to constructive values—without hearing stories that show the nobility and goodness of such things as honesty, heroism, kindness and generosity—children are vulnerable to the assumptions that cruelty is as valid as compassion, that selfishness is better than sacrifice, that greed is preferable to grace, that immediate gratification outshines an investment in the future.

On the other hand, the benefits of well-targeted, appropriate stories are many. Stories give shape to the chaotic world we experience. When children are familiar with stories—how they begin, develop, and end—they can fit their own experiences into story form and better interpret those experiences.

Psychiatrists say that seeing ourselves in the context of a larger story helps improve our chances of surviving traumatic experiences without psychological damage. It provides perspective for life. Adversity becomes something to overcome, not a reason to roll over and die. For this to be true, a child must be able to identify with the story.

Someone Like Me

I read recently about a man from the islands of Fiji who said, "When I was growing up, I was always looking for myself in a book. Of course, we had many attractive children's books from Australia, New Zealand and England. But never once did I see someone who looked like me walking across the pages."

Most of us have a similar hunger for "someone like me." Stories can satisfy this hunger, especially when they're told by a sensitive adult who understands children.

One of the principles I follow is that stories should speak *for* a child as much as they speak *to* a child. We don't always have to tell children what they need to hear or what they want to hear. At times the best thing is to tell children a story that *says* what they want to *say*.

Every listener has a story to tell. But, children, especially, may not have the vocabulary, the perspective or the ability to put their stories into a logical, coherent form. As storytellers, we can speak for them. It is a high compliment when our young listeners say, "Yes, yes! That happened to me" or "I felt the very same way."

This means our stories should present the world from a child's point of view. Characters in the story should react to situations the way a child would. They should also use language a child can understand.

Matching the language to the age level means more than not using advanced vocabulary. We also need to speak without being condescending. For example, with schoolchildren it's a mistake to refer to the ten-year-old protagonist as a "little" girl. Why? These children don't think of themselves as little children. Preschoolers, on the other hand, respond well to stories about "little" boys and girls. Why? Because that's how they see themselves. The language fits their age level.

The plots of your stories also need to fit the age level. One way to keep your stories on track is to ask yourself, "What is it like to be four?" (or whatever the age of the child you're telling stories to). Write down everything that comes to mind. Recall your own experiences at that age; imagine what today's youngsters are experiencing.

If your child is confronting something particular, consider "What is it like to go to school for the first time?" or "How does it feel to move to a new apartment?" or "What's it like having an older sister who is always faster, stronger and smarter?" What would you be thinking, feeling, fearing and enjoying in that situation? Spending five or ten minutes thinking sympathetically and empathetically along these lines will give you plenty of ideas for appropriate stories.

These thoughts can guide us as we try to match stories and styles to specific listeners or groups. But what *kinds* of stories are appropriate for each age level? How do tastes change as children grow older? When can imaginative stories start to supplement stories of concrete facts? These questions will be answered as we consider three particular age groups: 0-2 years old, 3-4 years old and 5-6 years old.

Ages 0-2: Impressions

Infants need human contact. Touch and tender sounds are more important than stimulating ideas. At this stage, children won't focus on a book, but they can concentrate on a familiar human face. They won't understand words, but they can begin to pick up the rhythms and intonation of speech. The best "storytelling" we can do for infants is through sensory impressions—warmth, comfort, security, touch.

Toddlers (ages 1-2) are ready to begin naming objects in their world. "This is your bed. I'm your mama. Here's your bottle." Children quickly learn key words, associating specific sounds with specific objects. By naming things, parents acquaint their children with the world, making it seem safer and more familiar. That's the beginning of storytelling.

Even two-year-olds can't sit still for long stories or comprehend fantasy, however. For them, the real world of people and things holds all the magic and mystery they need. "Stories" for this age often can be simple word-identification games. For instance, you can ask "Where's arm?" or "Where's thumb?" Children love figuring out what these words correspond to, pointing to their arm or thumb.

"Object" books are a great tool at this age. Object books picture various things common to a child's world—balls, cars, balloons, dogs, squirrels. With these, "storytelling" becomes sitting with the child, looking at the pictures and saying the words. After a while, the child will learn some of the words, and you can ask "Where's the squirrel?" and let the child point. Or ask "What's this?" pointing to one of the objects.

Other tools for this age are books that have little or no plot and merely follow a character through the day—from waking up to washing, dressing, eating, playing and going to bed. For toddlers, the fun comes in finding and naming the objects and action in the pictures.

You can tell stories that do verbally what object books do visually.

> Once there was a little boy named Joey. He liked to sleep under the covers. But in the morning, he would jump out of bed.
> Joey was thirsty. He wanted some milk. He went to the kitchen, and there, on the table, was a glass of cold milk. Just what he wanted!

Not a very complex plot. But it's enough to keep the interest of a toddler, who is still figuring out the basic pattern of life. From such simple stories, children will also learn what word will likely follow another—a big plus when they begin to read.

Ages 3-4: Independence and Imagination

Just about the time children have developed their ability to talk, they're also beginning to assert their independence. And stories on the theme of independence seem to be among the favorites at this age level, especially if the independence is firmly rooted in a dependable home life.

At this stage, children often ask for scary stories, but they still want everything to end happily. This interest in risk as well as security reflects a need to identify boundaries. Young children are trying to understand their own limitations, needs and fears. Through "safe scare" stories, children can discover their own delights and apprehensions and learn that other boys and girls feel the same way.

One natural source of story ideas for this age is to find out what the child is afraid of. Then, tell a story about *other* boys and girls who were afraid of the same thing. Learning that others are also afraid of bugs, for instance, can be a tremendous relief. Wise storytellers will make sure such stories have a reasonable amount of fear which then is relieved by a safe-and-sound ending.

Peter Rabbit by Beatrix Potter is perhaps the classic example. Peter asserts his independence and disobeys his mother, wandering into Farmer MacGregor's garden, where he is chased by a cat and Farmer MacGregor himself. He escapes in the nick of time, but he loses his coat and gets soaking wet. He must face the consequences.

By the time Peter returns home, he's sick. While his siblings Flopsy, Mopsy and Cottontail get to eat yummy blackberries, Peter has to drink chamomile tea. He (and the young listeners) experienced some anxious moments, but in the end everyone is satisfied by his return to the cozy rabbit home.

A second way the dependence/independence theme comes out is the three and four-year-olds' growing awareness of social relationships. Children reach out for playmates yet don't know how to relate to a friend. Parents sometimes think a child is being selfish when she refuses to share a ball or grabs all the pieces of a puzzle. Actually, the child isn't able, yet, to see anyone else's needs but her own. Through stories young children can see that other people have equally strong desires—stories about a child that learns to share, about the trials and joys of making friends.

A growing imagination is another major developmental step in this age group, and it emerges in several ways.

Imaginary friends. Many three-year-olds begin talking about a certain friend—and he or she will have a name: Jinx, Petey-Dink or some other creative concoction. This companion, invisible and inaudible to others yet inseparable from the child, takes part in conversations and even takes the blame for the child's mistakes and messes. In most cases, interest in imaginary friends will eventually just fade away as a child grows more confident with real life.

In our house, we started hearing about "Susan." Susan needed an extra place set for her at the table and was responsible whenever the milk was spilled. Later, "Max" appeared, and we played along.

These imaginary friends need not be debunked or belittled. They can be useful for parents and storytellers. One mother was told by her small daughter that the mess in the yard was caused by "Gemema" (the invisible friend). The mother replied, "You tell Gemema that she and you can't play in the yard again until both of you pick up the mess."

Such friends also can be a source of story ideas. Children enjoy hearing the exploits of themselves with their imaginary friends. The imaginary friend can be the child's rescuer or the child can free the imaginary friend from a perilous spot.

Pretending to be something else. At this stage, children often identify with certain animals. "I'm a hungry bear" you may hear, or "Grr—I'm a tiger." This interest can be put to use by storytellers who use animal protagonists in their stories. A story animal with a childlike personality may do things that might be threatening to the listener if a real child were doing them.

Small children in particular seem to have a natural identification with animals, especially dogs and cats. (One writer has suggested that "perhaps the simple lifestyle of the family dog is more akin to, and therefore more comprehensible, to the lifestyle of a three or four-year-old. Adult lifestyles often must seem fairly weird to a child of three.") For our daughter Stacey, her animal of choice was a cat. Our stories, by her request, inevitably involved the adventures of Stacey Cat, who might get lost and have to find her way back home or who might get chased by Bully Beagles and have to climb a tree.

Our daughter Kelsey's fascination was with worms, and she preferred stories about Kelsey Worm—who learned to sleep late, because "the early worm gets gotten by the early bird," and who loved to tunnel through gardens and scratch her back on carrots and potatoes.

Children at this stage are interested in real-life information as well as fantasy. Stories about animals, different occupations, different kinds of transportation, changing seasons and family life all have great appeal.

Ages 4-6: Interpretation

Children aged four through six continue to develop a growing independence and imagination. To these characteristics is added a growing need to interpret the world.

Going to school marks a turning point in children's lives.

But Are They Enjoying It?

Despite our preparation and knowledge of stories and techniques, storytelling ultimately comes down to this one question: Does my audience *like* it?

With children, the answer is as close as the expressions on their faces. In her book *Storytelling: Art and Technique,* Augusta Baker notes that "when children are enjoying a story their faces express interest, curiosity, delight.... A deep sigh and a faraway look at the end of the story usually mean that you have reached that child."

As Baker goes on to explain, we shouldn't be too eager to jump to conclusions about a story's impact: "Some children do not seem to be paying attention at all; yet these same children" may be the ones to request the very same story again and again.

For most, this is the first time away from the familiar world of home and family. Even if they've been in nursery school, children will tell you that "real school" is different: "You don't just play. There's work to do."

For these ages, stories that reflect a child's own journeys into the world are well-received. And, like the "safe scare" stories mentioned earlier, they are especially pleasing when an uncertain situation or adventurous day ends securely and happily.

The stories of Curious George, the mischievous monkey, are favorites because, through George, children assume a whole range of feelings and experiences. They sense danger and adventure, and they still get home safely.

Children also enjoy stories of realistic situations—stories about having arguments, being shy, feeling stupid. Beyond simply letting listeners know they aren't alone in their feelings, these stories can also present appropriate ways of handling those feelings.

With a growing independence and facility with words, children may also enjoy telling some stories of their own. Occasionally you may want to write down the story a child offers. Seeing spoken words transformed into lines and squiggles on paper helps kids see the connection between spoken and written words. Plus, by saving this masterpiece, you preserve thoughts and imagination that will be deeply appreciated later in life.

From Stories to Books

Shortly after age six, children start the transition to books. For a while, their powers of imagination will exceed their reading abilities. Because there is a great difference between what they can read and what they can listen to, understand and enjoy, children will still enjoy hearing stories that they would be unable to read themselves.

Eventually the transition to books will be complete. Unless, of course, you and your listeners enjoy stories so much that you'll make storytelling a habit. By then you will have developed your own favorites. You won't need any more help from me.

PART TWO

Stories You Can Use

The next seven chapters offer specific kinds of stories that you can use with children. Each chapter describes the importance of this type of story, offers some thoughts on how to tell this kind of story, illustrates with an actual story and then suggests several story starters.

These categories are certainly not exhaustive. I hope they spark other ideas for you. Here, at least, is enough material to stock your story repertoire for several weeks.

Each different literary genre has its worth. A fairy tale, or a story about the current superhero popular with children, may seem to have little educational value. Yet as long as the story respects the child and transmits an appreciation of basic values, it can help the child live a healthy emotional and spiritual life.

The stories themselves are easy to tell. Read them over a time or two, and the essential story line will stick in your head. The details are simple to recall or the plot develops in a clear pattern. This characteristic of being "readily retellable" was one of the main criteria used for selecting the stories in this book.

In addition, some of them communicate the character traits children need to develop. Others help with developmental skills. Others are just plain fun and let children and adults enjoy being together.

It isn't necessary to learn these stories word for word. If

you don't have all the details straight, no one will know the difference! In fact, if you tell the same story more than once, you'll find that it changes with each telling. A new character will appear or an old one will vanish, you'll tone down frightening incidents for the sake of sensitive children or elaborate on them for the sake of adventuresome listeners.

Whatever insertions or deletions have been made, the story itself remains. It has merely been shaped by the storyteller and adapted for its audience.

More importantly, the vital relationship between teller and listeners remains. That's the way it always has been with storytellers. That's the way it should be.

Chapter 5

"What If" Stories

Perhaps the easiest type of story to tell is the "what if" story. No research is needed—just a bit of imagination. These stories are only a premise away. Think of an unusual situation, and then think of what might happen if that situation were true.

To come up with such a premise, merely complete this sentence: "What would happen if...?"

What would happen if elephants could fly?

What would happen if you lived underwater?

What would happen if your nose grew every time you got angry?

What would happen if a train decided it didn't want to run on the tracks?

What would happen if you were invisible?

Each of these whimsical situations is a potential story. Actually, *several* stories. Each situation could be told from more than one viewpoint. For instance, the story of "What would happen if elephants could fly?" could be told from at least three viewpoints.

> Once there was an elephant named Ernest. He was exactly like all the other elephants except for one important difference. When he was very young, he discovered that if he spread his ears a certain way, he could fly!
>
> At first he was so excited that he tried to tell all the other elephants. They didn't believe him. So he showed them— looping and soaring into the sky. To his surprise, none of

Ernest's friends shared his excitement. In fact, they didn't like to see Ernest flying. They called him a showoff and a disgrace to all proper elephants.

Ernest was troubled. What should he do? Forget about flying? Fly only in secret? Or keep flying and hope that his family and friends would get used to it?

After thinking about it a bit, Ernest decided...

Or, the story could be told from the perspective of a nonflying elephant who encounters a flying elephant.

Eddie the elephant knew it was going to be a bad day. When he was walking to the river to cool off, suddenly he felt four heavy feet land on his back.

He wasn't near any trees, so he knew nothing could have jumped on him from the branches. No, this could mean only one thing: Ernest was up to his old tricks again.

Ernest was an elephant who had somehow learned to fly. He made it look so easy, swooping and soaring. He liked to play jokes on his friends, surprising them by silently landing on them when they least expected it, scaring them half to death. Never knowing when he might be used as a landing pad made Eddie nervous.

Eddie wished that he could fly, too, but couldn't get his fat, wrinkled body off the ground. Even when he tried to jump, he couldn't get all four feet up at the same time. But Eddie could do something that Ernest couldn't. And he decided to teach Ernest a lesson. So one day...

The story also could be told from the perspective of a human observer of flying elephants.

The most dangerous thing about living in Tuskville was the swarm of flying elephants that came buzzing in each year, just after the first rain. Other than that, it was a great place to live.

The first time Dietrich saw the elephants, he was amazed. They all landed on the roof of the bank. Even though the bank was a strong building, it came crashing down under the weight of the massive flock of elephants. People who lived in Tuskville said it was the same every year—much of the town was destroyed when the flying pachyderms hit town. And each year it got worse. More and more elephants were coming.

Dietrich knew something had to be done. And he had an idea. So one morning, when the town was quiet and no elephants were in sight...

Each of these "what if" situations could be developed in countless other directions. Flexibility is part of the advantage of "what if" stories.

These stories can be told briefly, with a quick and simple solution, or they can be developed into a more complex narrative involving several characters, additional complicating factors, and several unsuccessful attempts before a satisfactory conclusion is reached.

These stories also lend themselves to listener involvement. You can ask the children for ideas about how to resolve the problem and incorporate their thoughts into your story.

The story can become a parable, with an underlying theme of individuality, cooperation, kindness or courage. Or it can be simply an entertaining experiment in creativity that adults and children can share. Either way, this story form offers some strong benefits.

Here, for example, is one simple and quick bedtime story that our daughter Kelsey requested again and again. It was created during her "worm phase," when she was fascinated with the creatures that emerged whenever I dug in the yard.

Down in the soft, black dirt lived an earthworm named Clay. Clay was a very proud worm; he considered himself the fastest worm in the world. He'd never met a worm who could crawl faster than he. One day, however, Clay was wandering around in the dark, moist earth, not going anyplace in particular, when he almost bumped into the tail of a worm just in front of him.

"I'll zip right by him and show him my speed," said Clay, and he started crawling quickly through the soil. But the worm's tail in front of him picked up speed.

"Oh, so he thinks this is a race, huh?" said Clay. "I'll make tracks right over his back!" Faster and faster went Clay. But faster and faster went the worm in front of him. He couldn't catch up. Clay became angry. "I'm the fastest worm in the world," he told himself. He wanted to win the race even if he had to hurt the other worm to do it.

The other worm was right in front of him. Clay opened his mouth, and, with a mighty lunge, bit down on the tail as hard as he could.

"Yeeoww!" Clay screamed. The pain from his own tail suddenly stopped the race. The tail in front of him also stopped.

Then Clay realized that the tail he had been chasing was his own. He'd been crawling in a circle. His anger had caused him to bite himself in the tail. And now he was very, very sore.

How embarrassing.

That story was based on a girl's fascination with worms and the storyteller's wondering "what if" a worm, crawling underground, encountered its other end.

Story Starters

Here are a number of "what if" situations and a possible story starter for each. You can use the story starter, or you can take the "what if" situation and develop a completely different story. Or perhaps these will spark totally different ideas that you'd like to develop into your own stories.

What would happen if a skunk couldn't stink?

Once upon a time there was a little skunk who couldn't stink. No matter how hard he tried, he just couldn't do what seemed to be so easy for every other skunk. All the other skunks made fun of him, filling the air with their odor. But the skunk who couldn't stink just stood there wishing he could join in.

One day as he was thinking about his predicament...

What would happen if you fell into the world of the book you were reading?

Jessica loved to look at books, especially books that had pictures of trains. She could just imagine the smell of the smoke, the pounding of the engines, the back-and-forth rocking motion as the cars lumbered down the tracks.

Her favorite picture was of an old steam engine chugging

its way toward a mountain tunnel. There were some men on horseback near the tunnel entrance, watching the train approach. She wondered what they were doing.

As she looked, she felt a gust of wind against her face. The picture seemed to grow larger. The book in her lap disappeared, but the train was still there. Or, to be more precise, *she* was there. She could smell the smoke, hear the pounding engine, and feel the rocking motion. She stuck her head out the window. Yes, there was the tunnel. And there were the men on horseback. Jessica was *on* the train.

As the train neared the entrance to the tunnel...

What would happen to a lizard with no tail?

Once there was a lizard that lost its tail. He had no idea where it was. It had been there the night before, but when he woke up in the morning it was gone! He searched all around the rocks where he had been sleeping, but it was nowhere to be found.

He tried to make the best of the situation. After all, there was now less of him for the fierce birds of prey to grab with their claws. But that seemed a small comfort.

Then one evening, just before dark...

What would happen if nobody thought you were important, but you really were?

Jacob was the smallest kid in his school, and the other boys never let him forget it. They all were stronger, faster and taller. He wished he could do something better than any of them. And then one day he found out what it was. But he couldn't tell anyone. At least not yet. Jacob found out he could...

What would happen if a dinosaur showed up today?

Bayly the dinosaur crawled out of her familiar swamp and decided it was time to explore the rest of the world. After walking for what seemed like thousands of years, she found herself looking over the fence into the playground of the Main Street School. There the boys and girls were absolutely amazed to find a dinosaur standing next to the swings.

When one of the bravest girls politely asked if she would like to share part of her lunch, Bayly could only...

What would happen if creatures from outer space showed up at your front door?

Early one morning, before his parents awoke, David looked out the window and saw a large spaceship slowly land on the

street in front of him. Metal doors swung open and out march-
ed the strangest-looking creatures he had ever seen.

Then they rang the doorbell. David opened the door and...

It's also perfectly fair to take the intriguing premise of an
existing story and make up your own version, developing it
as you go along. For instance, take the situation presented in
the Russian fairy tale "To Your Good Health," and figure
out your own ending.

Long, long ago there lived a king who was such a mighty
monarch that whenever he sneezed everyone in the whole
country had to say, "To your good health!" Everyone said it
except the shepherd with the bright blue eyes, and he would
not say it because...

Or use the basic premise from a familiar story, and see how
you might treat it differently.

Once there was a family named Robinson that set sail on a
ship bound for a distant land. One night, a terrible storm arose,
and the ship started breaking up. The rest of the ship's passen-
gers tried to escape in small boats, but the Robinsons stayed,
alone.

In the morning, the family awoke to find the boat stuck on
the rocky coast of an island. Although they were all safe, the
Robinsons had no idea that they'd find...

All of these "what if" stories can incorporate elements of
past experience and personal interests, but they don't have to
be limited by them. The next category, however, focuses
specifically on the past experiences and personal backgrounds of you and your listeners.

Big Stories from a Simple Question

As examples of how a simple question of "What if?" can lead to an entertaining story, consider the following, simple ideas that resulted in some of our best-loved stories.

- What if a mermaid fell in love with a human? (*The Little Mermaid*, Hans Christian Andersen

- What if a hungry wolf came across three inventive pigs? ("The Three Little Pigs")

- What if a man so hated others that he decided to live under the sea? (*20,000 Leagues Under the Sea*, Jules Verne)

- What if there was a boy who never grew up? (*Peter Pan*, James Barrie)

- What if another world existed on the other side of your closet? (*The Lion, the Witch and the Wardrobe*, C. S. Lewis)

The basic premise behind these often-told stories is merely a "What if" question. From those two simple words have come a host of tales that have captured the imagination of generations.

Chapter 6

Family Tales

If "what if" stories develop a child's imagination, family tales shape a child's identity. Family stories help answer the questions "Who am I? Where do I come from? What makes me unique?"

I recently read an account by a Native American professor of literature in Southern California. When the professor was a small boy, his father awoke him early one morning and led him to the house of an old squaw. He left him there and said, "I'll come back for you this afternoon."

All day long the old Kiowa squaw told the boy stories, sang songs and described rituals to him. She told him the history of the Kiowa—how they began out of a hollow log in the Yellowstone River. She described wars with other tribes, great blizzards, buffalo hunts, the coming of white people, confrontations, fighting, moving southward to Kansas, deprivation, starvation, the diminished tribe and, finally, the Fort Sill reservation and a life of confinement.

When it was almost dark, the boy's father came and said, "Son, it's time to go." The son, many years later, remarked simply, "I left her house a Kiowa."

What had happened? In one sense, nothing—the boy just heard a story. In another sense, a life-changing event had occurred—he'd heard *his* story.

Keeping Family Stories in Mind

Like the Kiowan professor, Alex Haley, the author of *Roots* (Doubleday), was able to learn about his family from "living, walking archives of oral history." In Africa, the country of Haley's origin, these "walking archives" are known as *griots*.

When Haley visited Africa, he discovered that various kind of *griots* exist, from "seniors"—older men who commemorate special occasions by telling the stories of families, clans and heroes—to "apprentices"—younger men in training who repeatedly hear the tales of their people for as many as forty or fifty years.

Such storytellers are invaluable to their villages, for it is through them that each successive generation inherits the past, hearing oral histories that never diminish and always grow as the tales encompass each passing age.

Some of the greatest of these storytellers, Haley learned, can recount narratives of African history for three days—never repeating themselves. When he expressed astonishment at this fact, Haley was told that people who live in Western culture have conditioned themselves to "the crutch of print." Few Westerners, he was informed, really understand what human memory can accomplish.

Types of Family Tales

You most likely do not have a squaw nearby who can give a colorful account of your family history. But every family has a history worth passing along. Every child has a background worth discovering.

There are three types of personalized history that can be useful for creating family stories.

Relative truths. These are stories about kin, distant or close, living or dead, well-known or obscure. Almost every family has someone in the family tree to live up to—and someone to live down! As children grow, they should be introduced to both kinds of characters.

As far as I know, there's no one famous on either side of our family tree, but I've made sure our girls learned about their great-great grandfather Janzen. He came to America to escape the persecution of Mennonites in Russia in the late 1800s. In addition, they've learned that their great-great grandfather Haynes, as a boy, traveled with his family in a covered wagon from Tennessee to Texas. They found life in Texas so difficult that they loaded up the wagon and went back to Tennessee!

For many children, the extended family may not be nearby. Aunts and uncles, even grandparents, may be relative strangers. One of the best times for telling stories about these relatives is when you're traveling to see them. You can prepare children for a visit with their distant kin by telling whatever family stories you can remember—accounts drawn from earlier visits or stories passed down to you about that side of the family.

On our visits to Great-grandma Harrington, the girls usually ask for (and get) the family classic of how she and Great-granddad Harrington, before their wedding, were riding in the open rumble seat of a friend's car. When she got home, Great-grandma had a chipped tooth. Her family finally got her to confess the truth: it's risky to kiss in a rumble seat!

We also talk about looking for raccoons and opossum in the woods behind Great-grandma's house and feasting on the yeast rolls and comb honey that she loves to serve. The stories help build anticipation, help keep the girls close to Great-grandma and help maintain the identity that comes from being part of a family.

When I was your age. When children reach a certain age, they may not want to hear any more stories about Mom's childhood or Dad's growing up. In some circles, "When I was your age, I had to walk five miles to school, through snowdrifts, barefooted" has become an archetype for misguided parental attempts to relate stories of their personal history to their children.

But young children, I've found, enjoy occasional stories of Mom or Dad as a child—not necessarily stories where the parent comes across as heroic or a model child, but stories in which the parent is less than perfect, someone they can identify with. Perhaps it's a sign of innate perversity, but they especially seem to enjoy episodes in which the main character did something wrong and gets punished or hurt. In our house, one of the girls' favorite stories is my wife's account of the time she was riding a horse. The girth broke, the saddle slipped and Susan fell from the horse, breaking her arm.

The girls also enjoy hearing about my father spanking me for refusing my mother's request to eat two green beans left on my plate. (The green beans were a side issue, I now realize. My father's action was more in response to my attitude toward my mother's request than to the number of vegetables remaining.)

Kids enjoy these kinds of stories, I suspect, because they find it comforting to know their parents made mistakes as kids. Now that we're parents, maybe we'll be more understanding of their shortcomings.

Yes, it's good too for children to hear about their parents' achievements and successes. Those seem to come across better, however, when told by a grandparent, uncle or some other relative who can be encouraged (or bribed!) to tell stories showing your better side.

When you were small. Children don't have to be very old before they'll enjoy stories about their own earlier years. Knowing there are true stories in which they play the main role seems to boost their self-esteem and give them a feeling of significance.

When Stacey was eighteen months old, she went with me to the grocery store. She didn't like to be confined to the child-seat portion of the grocery cart, however. I soon tired of her cries and let her stand in the larger cargo section of the cart.

As we finished shopping and I pushed the cart toward our car, I didn't see the crack in the asphalt. The cart lurched to a sudden stop. Stacey, who had been standing at the front, fell forward, face first. The dull scrunch of her skull hitting the pavement sent panic through me. For a sickening moment there was silence. *I killed her!* I thought. Then she screamed. Mixed feelings of relief, fear and desperation churned inside.

I scooped her up, held her tightly to my chest and babbled unthinkingly, "Oh, Stacey, Stacey. It's okay, it's okay, it's okay." I desperately hoped it would be.

Quickly I threw the two bags of groceries into the car, laid Stacey in the front seat beside me and headed for the nearest hospital. She eventually stopped crying, but she crawled onto my lap and held tightly to my neck. I prayed aloud for her recovery as we pulled up to the emergency entrance.

The nurses dressed her abrasions, the doctors ordered x-rays of her skull and checked for concussion. Fortunately, no serious injury had been sustained.

For several months after that, every time we passed the store where the accident occurred, Stacey wanted to hear the story. I obliged. It was my way of working through the trauma of a close call, and I figured it might be her way too. I concluded by saying that "Stacey was very brave. God answered our prayer. And Daddy will always be more careful and not let that happen again."

It was a horrible experience, but it has had positive effects. Several years now have passed, but periodically Stacey refers to that event, her perception influenced by the telling and retelling of the story. Stacey's identity has been shaped by the event. She knows she was brave, that God and the doctors took care of her, and that her daddy was there. She has the story to prove it.

Story Starters

As you think about the three kinds of family stories described above, I hope some of your own memories will be
stirred.

Stories about relatives are dependent upon how well you
know them and what stories have been passed down to you.
Stories about your own childhood and the experiences of
your children, however, can be recalled by considering
some key questions.

Following are several story-starting thoughts that might
bring some of your own stories to mind. For each question,
think through your experiences. Then recall your children's
experiences. What episodes have been, or could be, influential in shaping your child's identity?

The first set of questions deals with memorable events.
What specific events have been most influential in making
you the person you are and in making your children the
people they are?

- I remember one of our best vacations was the time we...
- One of the biggest messes you ever made...
- The time you were most scared...
- The time you were most glad to be part of this family...
- The first time you *[choose one]* saw snow, went swimming,
  ate ice cream, rode a bike, brushed your own teeth, or...

Another type of story centers on character traits you
would like the child to develop.

One of the best ways of encouraging particular traits is to
tell children stories drawn from their own lives that posit-
ively evidence those traits. These stories can come from
"when you were small," but they don't have to be based
on distant memories; they can be as recent as this morning.

- I realized you were a unique individual when I saw you...
- I was so glad you were in my family when you...
- Once when you got hurt, you had to be brave...
- I could tell you were kind when you...
- I was so proud of you when...

● You accomplished something I didn't think you could do when...

The stories that emerge from your own family lore can become a special treasure to hand down to your children. It's an inheritance you both can enjoy.

Chapter 7

Classics Retold

What do the following expressions have in common: "That's just sour grapes," "What a Herculean task," "Hers was a Cinderella existence," "Don't be such a Scrooge"?

Do you recognize the link? They're all expressions that come out of classic literature—fables, myths, folktales and time-tested stories. Quotations, plots and people from the classic stories furnish us with much of the script for our lives.

Consider these words and phrases: *rags to riches, Cheshire grin, Chicken Little, days of Camelot, Oedipus complex, Big Brother is watching, a comedy of errors, playing Cupid, crying "wolf,"* and *"Bah, humbug."* Each of these takes on greater meaning when we recognize the allusion. There's a story behind many of our common expressions, and to know the story is to understand better the expression.

In 1987 E. D. Hirsch, Jr., published a book that sparked extensive discussion throughout the United States. Titled *Cultural Literacy: What Every American Needs to Know,* the book points out that communication requires a shared understanding, that speaking the language requires more than words.

Today's general information sources—magazines, newspapers, television reports—assume a prior knowledge of certain events, people and places. Hirsch argues that a person who thinks the Alamo is an epic poem by Homer, that Socrates was a Native American chieftain, or that the Great

Gatsby was a magician is *functionally* illiterate. He suggests that large numbers of people today, though they are technically able to read, are unable to understand their world because of gaps in their cultural literacy.

Telling stories to children is certainly not the complete solution for this situation. But by using some of the classic tales, we can take a significant step in the right direction.

Three Benefits of Using Classic Stories

Throughout the centuries, each generation has learned the history, mythology, values, and the moral and religious heritage of its culture through stories. There are at least three additional reasons to use classics as the basis for stories.

Classics provide a means for understanding and expressing ourselves. In later years, your children will be glad they've been exposed to the characters and stories that have been the foundation of culture and civilization over the generations. They'll be glad they heard the stories of Peter Pan, the Pied Piper, and the tales of the Brothers Grimm—because chances are, they will be referred to again in the future.

Classics help children deal with life's central ideas—life and death, good and evil, wisdom and foolishness, sacrifice and perseverance, victory and defeat. It's easy for a child to grow up without confronting these ultimate issues. As adults, we do children no favor by allowing them to avoid the truly significant subjects. Classic stories are one way of introducing children to these important concepts.

Most classics can easily be adapted into oral versions that children enjoy. In fact, many of the classics that we think of as children's stories were not originally intended exclusively for children. At the time, they were everyone's entertainment. Cinderella, for instance, complete with glass slipper, can be traced back to Egyptian legend. Many of the early novels, such as *Robinson Crusoe* and *Gulliver's Travels,* were written for adults and later adapted for and adopted by children.

Not until the 1740s did specifically juvenile literature emerge in a significant way. Entrepreneur John Newbery produced the first children's book designed to entertain as well as teach. The modern Newbery Award for significant children's literature was named after him. And such children's literature stands alongside the timeless classics as a good source of storytelling material.

Children's literature has gone through stages and fads. At times it was heavy on morals and graphic on the wages of sin. At other times it has been sentimental and sweet, with fairy tales condemned as too violent. At still other times, realistic life situations were the rage. Whatever the thrust, children's literature has continued to be a prime means of entertaining and orienting a new generation.

Such literature can also be a source of story ideas. Good children's stories are not weaker, watered-down versions of adult literature. They are equally significant and perhaps more-powerful transmitters of the culture and values of civilization. An added benefit: many adults enjoy renewing their own acquaintance with the stories they dimly remember from their own growing-up years.

Dealing with Two Difficulties

With some of the classics, storytellers run into two obstacles. Neither, however, is insurmountable.

First, many of these stories require some explanation. Perhaps the setting (a sultan's harem, for instance) is completely foreign. This does not mean the story should be avoided. It simply means the necessary information should be given before telling the story.

At times an unfamiliar word or phrase may be crucial to understanding the story. Storyteller Caroline Feller Bauer tells of one such case.

One of my favorite stories is Isaac Bashevis Singer's "The First Schlemiel" in his *Zlateh the Goat* (Harper, 1966). In New York I told the story many times and to everyone's great amusement. The first time I told it in Oregon, it didn't get the same reaction. Much to my dismay, I discovered that many Oregonians didn't know the meaning of the word *schlemiel*. I puzzled about how to introduce the story in the future. At last I found a way that involved teaching the audience two Yiddish terms instead of one. "The difference," I now explain, "between a schlemiel and a schlimazel is that a schlemiel is the kind of guy who is always spilling the soup, and a schlimazel is the guy he spills it on."

Such pitfalls can be avoided early on by looking out for any potential problem words or phrases and making the appropriate introductions. Such introductions can be as simple as asking "Do all of you know what a hippopotamus is?" or "What does a mermaid look like?" (This has the added benefit of immediately sparking interest in the story to come.)

A second obstacle is the dark and sometimes bloody descriptions in some of the stories. Many people have objected to folktales because of the morbid themes or violence. It's true that many are unsuitable for younger children. Some offer low ideals or a false view of life. Many others, upon closer inspection, can be seen simply as portrayals of the struggle between good and evil. The triumph of good over evil comes out through some sort of sacrifice, but rarely is it presented with the gore emphasized in movies and comic books.

In "The Seven Ravens," for instance, a sister is searching for her seven bewitched brothers who have been turned into birds. At a crucial moment, the sister cuts off her finger to use as a key to open the door of a glass mountain. This act symbolizes her sacrifice in exchange for love and forgiveness. In addition, it is overshadowed by the brothers' return to their human form and their reunion with their sister.

If a child seems to be frightened by a story, it should

probably be adapted, substituting less disturbing details. The purpose of a story is the listener's enjoyment, not terror. Some of these fairy tales can wait until the child is older.

Types of Classics

Among the classics—the stories that are part of our popular literary tradition—there are several different categories. Each contains abundant material that can be adapted into stories for children. Many fables, myths, and folk and fairy tales indirectly present lessons in good behavior that both you and your listeners will enjoy.

Tips for Telling Classic Stories

The following basic guidelines will enhance your storytelling and spark listener involvement.

- *Show enthusiasm.* If you are excited about the story you're telling, listeners will mirror your enthusiasm. Vary the tone of your voice; make the story feel "alive."

- *Show emotion.* Hold long descriptions to a minimum and concentrate on the feelings of your characters. Be mindful of the emotions your characters are experiencing and reflect them in your voice and facial expressions.

- *Maintain eye contact.* This applies even if you're reading from a storybook. Keeping your eyes on your audience will not only heighten listeners' involvement with the story, it will alert you to restlessness or other signals that require a change of pace in your story.

- *Avoid distractions.* Pacing back and forth or interjecting "uh" or "um" will draw attention to you—and away from your story. Relax. If you get stuck, ask your listeners what might happen next and proceed from there.

Fables

Many fables indirectly offer readers and listeners solid lessons in good behavior. A recurring theme in Aesop, for instance, is that pride leads to failure. Here are just a few of the fables that can be reviewed and then told extemporaneously to children, providing vivid pictures of right and wrong without preaching.

The Shepherd's Boy and the Wolf

A mischievous shepherd's boy used to amuse himself by calling, "Wolf! Wolf!" just to see the villagers run with their clubs and pitchforks to help him. He did this more than once as a joke, laughing at the villagers each time, and the villagers grew angry.

One day a wolf really did sneak in among the sheep. The boy called "Wolf! Wolf!" in vain. The villagers went on with their work, the wolf killed as many sheep as it wanted, and the shepherd's boy learned that liars are not believed—even when they do tell the truth.

The Crow and the Pitcher

A thirsty crow, after looking in vain for water to drink, at last saw some in the bottom of a pitcher. Seeing this water made him more thirsty than ever, and he began to think how he could get it. He finally had a plan. By dropping pebbles into the pitcher until he brought the water near the top, he had all he wanted. Then he said to himself, "Well, I know now that little by little does the trick."

The Hare and the Tortoise

A hare was once boasting about how fast he could run, when a tortoise, overhearing him, said, "I'll race you!" "Fine," said the hare, laughing to himself. "But let's get the fox for a judge." The fox agreed and the race began.

The hare quickly outran the tortoise. Knowing he was far ahead, he lay down to take a nap. "I can easily pass the tortoise when I wake up," he told himself.

Unfortunately, the hare overslept. When he awoke, though he ran his best, he discovered that the tortoise already had finished. He learned that "slow and steady wins the race."

Mythology

Technically speaking, myths are the traditional stories of preliterate cultures that concentrate on the exploits of supernatural gods and goddesses, great ancestors and larger-than-life heroes. Although Greek and Roman myths are probably the most familiar to us, they are by no means the only myths. Nearly every culture has a rich history of mythical lore from which storytellers can draw.

Here is a brief sampling of the kinds of myths that can be read and then presented as stories to children.

Icarus and Daedelus

Daedelus and his son, Icarus, were prisoners on an island far out at sea. There, the king's soldiers made sure no prisoners escaped by hiding in ships or swimming away.

Daedelus was clever. As he watched the seagulls fly, he had an idea. He gathered all the feathers he could find, large and small. He sewed them together and shaped them into wings with wax. Fastening the wings onto his arms, he practiced with them until he could fly. Next he made a set of wings for Icarus and taught him how to use them.

"Be sure not to fly too high or too low," he warned his son. "If you get too low, the spray from the waves will make the wings heavy. If you fly too high, the sun will melt the wax, and the wings will fall apart."

Then came the day for their escape. Daedelus and Icarus took off, soaring into the sky toward freedom. Daedelus flew straight toward their home, but Icarus wanted to see how high he could fly.

"Come down," called his father. "Follow me!" But Icarus didn't listen. He flew higher and higher. As he got closer to the sun, the air got warmer and warmer. The wax softened, and his wings started drooping. Still Icarus soared higher.

Suddenly the feathers came apart. With a cry of terror, Icarus fell like a leaf tossed by the wind. He tumbled out of the sky and into the sea, where no one could help him.

Daedelus heard his son's cry and flew back to find him. All he found were a few feathers floating on the water, and he realized that his disobedient son had drowned. Sadly, he flew on to the nearest land, which he named Icaria in honor of his son. There he hung up his wings. Never again did he fly.

Damon and Pythias

Long ago, there were two young men named Damon and Pythias, who were best friends. One day, the king became so angry at Pythias that he ordered him to be locked up in prison until the day he would be put to death.

Before going to prison, however, Pythias wanted first to say good-bye to his father and mother, who lived in a faraway part of the kingdom. He begged the king to let him go, but the king refused.

"If I let you go," said the king, "you will never come back."

Then Damon said, "If you let Pythias say good-bye to his father and mother, I will take his place in prison until he returns."

"What if he doesn't come back?" said the king.

"Then I will die in his place," said Damon.

The king agreed. Damon went to prison and Pythias began his journey home, promising to come back as soon as he could.

Day after day went by, and Pythias did not return. At last the time came for Pythias to be killed, and still he did not return. Because of the agreement the friends had made, the soldiers came to Damon's prison cell and took him outside to die.

Just then Pythias came running up. His ship had been wrecked. He'd had to swim to land and walk the rest of the way back to the prison. The king, who never expected to see Pythias again, was amazed.

"Why did you come back to die?" he asked. "You could have been free by staying away."

"I told you I would come back," said Pythias. "I hurried as fast as I could because I was afraid Damon would have to die in my place."

The king was so impressed that he changed his mind. "Pythias shall live!" he announced. "And Damon shall be free! Such true friends are worth more than all the world."

Folk and Fairy Tales

Folktales often center around one person, animal or group. At times these characters are witty; at other times they're dimly witted. In most cases, they're ordinary people and ordinary animals (unless you consider talking animals extraordinary). Fairy tales often add the element of enchantment, and they usually involve princesses, kings, queens, cruelty and romantic love.

Each part of the world has developed its own set of classic folktales and fairy tales. From England, the stories of Robin

Hood, King Arthur, Saint George and the Dragon, and Jack and the Beanstalk have become familiar around the world. In the United States, Br'er Rabbit is a traditional favorite. In Germany, Jakob and Wilhelm Grimm collected folktales they heard from peasants and published them in 1812. Although not all of the Grimm tales are appropriate for children, many have been consistently popular, including "Hansel and Gretel," "Rapunzel," "Rumpelstiltskin."

Some folktales are droll and humorous. For instance, in Jewish folklore, there is a mythical town called Chelm, in which all the inhabitants are stupendously stupid. Stories about Chelm can be found in several collections (including *Zlateh the Goat* by Isaac Bashevis Singer). Here's a typical story of the citizens of Chelm:

> Once the people of Chelm thought they could make money by selling lumber from the mountain that overlooked their town. For weeks the men of Chelm chopped down the largest trees and cut off the branches until they had a fine pile at the top of the mountain. Then it took a month for the men to lift and carry the great tree trunks down the mountain. At last the huge job was almost done.
>
> Two strangers arriving in town on the last day watched in amusement as the men carried the logs down the mountain.
>
> "Why don't you just roll the logs down instead of carrying them?" asked one of the strangers.
>
> "What a good idea!" exclaimed the men of Chelm. "Let's do it." And with that they began the long trek back up the mountain, each man hauling a log so that when he reached the top he could roll it down.

There are many other tales that are appropriate for telling to children. Here is another example, which comes from India.

The Tiger, the Brahman and the Jackal

One day a man from India, called a Brahman, found a fierce tiger locked in a cage. "Let me out," growled the tiger. "Oh, no," said the Brahman. "If I did, you would eat me."

"Certainly not!" said the tiger. "I would thank you all my

life." And then the tiger cried so sadly that the Brahman felt sorry for him and opened the cage.

Quickly the tiger leaped out and said, "How foolish you are. I will eat you for my dinner." The Brahman was frightened, but he said, "Is this any way to repay my kindness? Let's ask the next two creatures we see what would be fair." The tiger agreed.

The first creature to come by was a water buffalo. "This tiger wants to eat me," said the Brahman. "Is that fair?"

"Men make me pull heavy loads all day and feed me only scraps," said the buffalo. "The tiger treats you like men treat me. You should expect him to eat you."

The tiger laughed. The Brahman was unhappy, and he waited for the next creature to come by.

Then came a jackal, a sly animal. When the Brahman told his story, the jackal pretended to be all mixed up. "You mean you were in the cage, and the tiger found you?"

"No!" shouted the tiger. "I was in the cage."

"I'm sorry," said the jackal. "I get so confused. Of course, I was in the cage, and..."

"No!" roared the tiger. "It was *I* who was in the cage."

"I'm sorry," said the jackal again. "This is too hard to understand. Dear me. How could you get in the cage?"

"I'll make you understand," growled the angry tiger, and he jumped into the cage to show the jackal how he got in.

"Oh, *now* I understand," said the jackal, as he quickly slammed the cage door shut. The tiger was caught again, and the kind Brahman was saved, thanks to the quick-thinking jackal.

The classic stories suggested in this chapter are just a few of the possibilities. Plenty of others can be found in anthologies of children's literature in your local bookstore or library. There are also two other types of stories that are, in a sense, classics: Bible stories and historical episodes. Each of those categories deserves its own chapter.

Chapter 8

Stories from the Bible

Not long ago, I was pulling weeds from between the rows of corn and beans in our garden. It was hot, sticky work. As I paused to wipe my face, I saw two neighborhood children standing next to the fence watching me.

"I guess we have Adam and Eve to thank for having to pull all these weeds, don't we?" I said.

The two children looked blank.

"Have you ever heard of Adam and Eve?"

They both shook their heads no. I was surprised, but I sensed an opportunity to leave the weeds for a while and do something much more enjoyable: tell a story. I could justify it as one small skirmish with cultural illiteracy.

"Would you like to hear the story of how Adam and Eve got thrown into the weeds?" I asked. The two kids nodded eagerly. So I launched into the story.

> Way back at the very beginning of time, there were two people, Adam and Eve, who lived in a beautiful garden full of fruits and vegetables and absolutely no weeds. God put them there and gave them permission to eat from everything in the garden—their choice—except for one tree. The fruit from that tree was like poison, and God knew that Adam and Eve would die if they ate it.
>
> So Adam and Eve enjoyed the garden. They had plenty of time to enjoy it because they never had to pull weeds. But then, a serpent entered the garden. It told Eve she ought to eat from the one tree she wasn't supposed to.

At first Eve said no, that there were plenty of other trees to eat from. But the serpent kept saying, "Why not?" He got Eve to stop thinking about the many trees she could eat from and to think mostly about the one tree she was supposed to avoid. The serpent told her, "Go ahead. You won't die. In fact, eating from that tree will make you wiser."

Eve at last took a bite of the forbidden fruit, and then Adam walked by. He ate some too. They didn't die right then, but suddenly they knew something was very, very wrong. They felt something inside that they'd never felt before.

That evening, God came to the garden, and he couldn't find Adam and Eve. They were hiding in the bushes. They looked guilty, and God knew they'd done something wrong.

"Did you eat from the tree I told you to stay away from?" God asked.

Adam and Eve said yes, that they had done what the serpent told them to do.

For their disobedience, God sent Adam and Eve out of the beautiful garden. They had to go to a place where Adam had to work by the sweat of his brow. He had to grow their food in the middle of the weeds.

Ever since, we've had trouble with weeds.

You don't find it exactly that way in the biblical book of Genesis but, under the circumstances, it was close enough. Several weeks later, I asked the two kids if they remembered Adam and Eve. "Sure," they said. "They were the ones kicked out of the garden and into the weeds." It wasn't a comprehensive understanding, but I felt it was a small step toward cultural literacy.

The Old and New Testaments offer a wealth of stories about both rogues and role models: Queen Jezebel and Queen Esther, Delilah and Deborah, Samson and Samuel, Judas and Jesus. Many of the characters are as distinctive as any contemporary superhero. Consider John the Baptist, dressed in animal skins and eating locusts and wild honey while telling the world that Jesus was coming. Or Joseph, sold as a slave by his brothers, imprisoned on false charges by his master's wife, freed after interpreting a dream, rising to

The Value of Bible Stories

Many children today have never heard the stories of the Bible. Yet, like the classics mentioned in chapter 7, Bible stories are an important part of our literary and historical tradition.

Not only are holidays such as Christmas and Easter, and concepts such as the Ten Commandments and the Golden Rule, still prominent, but our contemporary language is peppered with phrases that come from the Bible:

"Burning the midnight oil."

"The handwriting is on the wall."

"Weighed in a balance."

"An eye for an eye, and a tooth for a tooth."

"Turn the other cheek."

"Throwing pearls before swine."

"He has the patience of Job."

"Eat, drink and be merry..."

Not only are the stories behind these phrases significant and memorable, but they're full of intrigue, action, suspense—traits that make them easier to tell to children. Children, especially those hearing the stories for the first time, are certain to be entertained.

In addition, knowing the significance of such things as a shibboleth, a golden calf, the land of milk and honey, being born again, thirty pieces of silver and Armageddon is, according to E.D. Hirsch, Jr., essential for participating in public discourse. Knowing the stories behind these allusions helps us communicate.

become "vice-pharaoh" and playing a trick on his brothers even while he's saving their lives.

Adapting Bible Stories for Kids

Some parents read these stories to their children straight out of the Bible itself. This method, for some children, can be effective, especially if you use a simplified version such as

The Living Bible (Tyndale House), *The International Children's Bible* (Word) or *The Lion Story Bible* (Lion Publishing).

Other adults find their young listeners have greater attention and retention when they adapt the stories, telling them much as they would any other story, using the biblical material as the basic story line. By adapting Bible stories, storytellers can take into account the varying interests and levels of understanding of their listeners.

Some children, for instance, might want to hear only about the action—the three young Hebrews who refused to bow to the king's statue and were then thrown into a fiery furnace. Others enjoy the descriptive little details—what kinds of vegetables Daniel and his friends wanted to eat and what kinds of rich foods he turned down.

If it helps children follow the story, I don't think it's inappropriate to speculate. So, in the case of Daniel's menu, the good foods might have been beans, corn, apricots and chick peas, while the rich foods might have been sausages and cakes.

Adapted Stories from the Bible

Here are two Bible stories that have been adapted for young children. Additional stories are available in books of Bible stories available in most bookstores. Many of these books are richly illustrated with pictures that help children visualize the unique setting of the biblical episodes.

Queen Esther

In the land of Babylon lived a beautiful girl named Esther. One day some men came to Esther's town—announcing that King Xerxes was looking for the most beautiful woman in the kingdom to be his queen. When they saw how beautiful Esther was, they took her back to the palace of their king. King Xerxes, too, recognized her beauty and chose her to be his new queen.

One of the king's friends was a proud and evil man named

Haman, who wanted people to bow down whenever he drove by. Esther's cousin Mordecai, however, would not bow down to Haman. This made Haman so angry that he decided to kill Mordecai and all of his people.

Mordecai told Esther of Haman's plans. "You could be killed too," he told his cousin the queen. "You must try to save us."

"But Haman is the king's friend," said Esther. "And the king is sometimes a cruel man. He might kill me himself if I make him upset. How can I save us?"

Nevertheless, after asking Mordecai and all her people to pray, Esther agreed to try. She asked King Xerxes to come to a special dinner she had made for him. There she served all the king's favorite foods. Xerxes was pleased with Esther's delicious dinner.

Esther summoned her courage and finally spoke. "Please don't be angry with me. Someone is trying to kill me and all my people. And that person is a friend of yours."

"Who?" asked the king. Esther was afraid of the king, but she told him the truth.

"It is Haman."

Instead of being angry at Esther, the king was angry at Haman. He ordered his soldiers to capture Haman and hang him on the very gallows he had made for Mordecai.

Esther's beauty and bravery saved her people.

Samson and Delilah

There once lived a man named Samson. God promised to make him the strongest man in the land and to protect his people from their enemies. To receive these promises, Samson was told never to cut his hair. And although Samson was very strong, sometimes he was foolish. He did not obey God.

He fell in love with Delilah, a woman who was an enemy of Samson's people. Her friends begged her to learn the secret of Samson's strength, so she could make him weak and they would be able to capture him. She pleaded with Samson, "Please tell me, what makes you so strong?"

Samson teased her. "If you tie me with new ropes, I won't have the strength to fight." So when Samson went to sleep that night, Delilah tied him with new ropes. Then she woke him up, saying, "Samson! Your enemies are here to attack you!"

He jumped up, snapped the ropes easily and looked around for the enemies. But no one else was there. It had been Delilah's way of testing Samson's story about the ropes.

"Samson, you didn't tell me the truth," Delilah said, pretending to be upset. "You don't love me."

Finally Samson told her the truth: if she cut his hair, his strength would be gone. That night, when he was asleep, Delilah cut his hair. Then she called her friends to capture him. Samson was powerless. His enemies grabbed him and blinded him. They threw him in a prison.

Samson was sorry for what he had done. He asked God to forgive him for disobeying and telling Delilah his secret. Slowly his hair grew back, but his eyes still could not see.

One day his enemies were having a big dinner and they wanted to make fun of Samson in front of all their guests. They brought him to a huge temple where everyone could see him and laugh at him.

At Samson's request, his captors allowed him to stand between two pillars that held up the roof. He prayed for strength, and God made his muscles strong one last time. Samson pressed his hands against the pillars and pushed with all his might. The tall, stone pillars cracked, and the roof came crashing down, burying Samson and all of his enemies beneath the stones.

The following stories, adapted from Mary Batchelor's *The Children's Bible in 365 Stories* (Lion Publishing), exemplify the kind of stories that can be drawn from Jesus' life as it was recorded in the New Testament.

The Enormous Picnic

Jesus and his twelve disciples were very tired after telling many large crowds about God. One day, Jesus suggested that they all go off for a short rest.

The disciples thankfully agreed, and they all clambered into Peter's boat and set off across a lake. But as they drew nearer to the land on the other side, they saw that the quiet spot they were heading for was now full of people.

The people were all waiting for their first glimpse of Jesus. They had seen the boat leave and had raced around the shore, arriving on the other side ahead of Jesus and his disciples.

Seeing the crowds, the disciples were disappointed, but Jesus saw the crowds as people in need of his loving care. All day long he taught the people about God.

When evening came, the disciples were very tired. "Send the crowds away," they begged. "It's dinner time, and there are no shops here. They'll have to hurry if they are to get to town in time to buy food."

"Why don't *you* give them a meal?" Jesus asked.

"How could we do that?" Philip asked. "It would cost a small fortune to feed so many people. There must be over five thousand people here."

Then Andrew spoke up.

"There's a boy here who has offered us his lunch. But it's only two little fish and five small bread rolls. What can we do with it?"

Jesus did not answer Andrew's question right away. Instead, he said, "Sort the people into groups of fifty. Then get them to sit down on the grass."

As the disciples bustled off to organize everyone, Jesus turned to the boy, who was waiting nearby. "Thank you," Jesus said with a smile, as he accepted the boy's meal of fish and bread.

When everyone was ready and waiting, Jesus held up the picnic food for all to see, and he thanked God for it. And then something incredible happened.

The bread and fish that Jesus handed to each disciple to give to the crowd was more than enough for all of the people! Even the children had to say, "I'm full!" at last. In fact, twelve baskets full of food were left over at the end of the meal!

Jesus not only wanted the people to know about God, he wanted them to have enough food to eat.

The parables—or "teaching stories"—that Jesus often used when questioned by his followers provide easy-to-understand stories with solid moral foundations. Found in the New Testament books of Matthew, Mark, Luke and John, parables can be adapted easily for listeners of various ages and backgrounds.

The Good Friend

Long ago, Jesus was asked, "What does it mean to love other people?" He decided to answer the man's question by telling a story.

"One day," Jesus began, "a Jewish man set off down the steep and dangerous road from Jerusalem to Jericho. Suddenly robbers sprang on him from behind some large boulders. They beat him, stole his clothes and money, then ran away—leaving him half-dead by the roadside.

"After a while, someone else came along. He was a Jewish priest who was walking home after doing his work at the temple in Jerusalem. When he saw the injured man lying by the side of the road, he was afraid. He walked quickly past, staying on the other side of the road. For all he knew, the man might be dead; no priest was supposed to touch a dead body.

"A little later, a second man came along. He too had been serving God in the Jewish temple. When he spotted the injured man, he crossed the road to have a closer look. He easily guessed what had happened to the man. But then he wondered to himself, 'What if the robbers are still around, hiding behind the rocks, waiting to jump on *me?* What if this is a trick to steal all of my money?' Frightened, this man hurried off quickly.

"At last, a man from the town of Samaria came along. Now, Jews and Samaritans usually had nothing to do with each other. For as long as anyone could remember, the two groups had despised each other.

"But this Samaritan felt full of pity for the injured man. It didn't make any difference to him that the man was different from himself. He went over to the man and began to clean up his wounds. He covered the man's cuts and bruises with soothing oil and bandaged him up. Then he carefully lifted him onto his donkey and took him to the nearest inn to rest.

"The Samaritan gave the innkeeper two silver coins and said, 'Take good care of him until he is well. If you have any further expense, I'll pay you the next time I come by.'

After telling the story, Jesus turned to his questioner. "Which of the three passersby showed love to the wounded man?" he asked.

"The one who was kind to him, I suppose," the man admitted.

"Then go and be like him," Jesus said.

These are just a few examples of the kinds of stories in the Bible. Not all of them are sweet, everyone-lives-happily-ever-after stories. But the stories are powerful accounts of the consequences of people's choices, stories that have shaped hundreds of generations.

Chapter 9

Historic Tales

"History is bunk," according to American automobile man-ufacturer Henry Ford. But those of us who have been en-thralled by the stories of history would argue that point. The momentous occasions of the past offer stories of bravery and cowardice, victory and failure, greatness and greed.

Like familiarity with the classics, knowledge of history deepens our understanding of the modern world. And like the many well-known quotations from the Bible, historical references inhabit our popular phrases:

"He met his Waterloo."

"Beware the ides of March."

"It was a Pyrrhic victory."

"That was his last stand."

"*Et tu, Brute?*"

"What is this, an inquisition?"

Even terms like *marathon* and *Spartan existence* take on additional weight when understood as part of great stories out of history. Knowing those stories helps us avoid the snobbery which assumes our day is the only day.

Thus, history becomes a vast source of stories and char-acters ready-made for your own telling. Stories can be found in actual accounts in history books (and some of these stories are found at the end of this chapter), but history is also full of legends, which can be adapted and amplified for young listeners.

Historic Docudrama

Once, when our family was driving through Kentucky and I was trying to keep the girls from getting too rambunctious, I pointed to the forests along the road and asked about the most famous person I could think of connected with Kentucky.

"Did I ever tell you a story about Daniel Boone, who lived in the Kentucky woods—just like those?"

The next several miles were taken up with legends (many of them just minutes old) about the famous frontiersman. For instance:

Once there was a man named Daniel Boone, who lived deep in the Kentucky woods. One song about him said, "Daniel Boone was a man—yes, a big man—with an eye like an eagle and as strong as a mighty oak tree."

One day Daniel Boone was walking through the woods when he heard a howl behind him. He knew it was a wolf! Then he heard another. And another. A whole pack of wolves was following him, just out of sight behind the trees. And they didn't sound like friendly wolves.

Daniel Boone started running. He ran as fast as he could. When he stopped and listened, he still heard the howls of the wolves. They were getting closer. They were sounding hungrier!

When he turned to run again, he quickly came to a stop. In front of him was a wide, deep river—too deep to swim across.

But Daniel Boone was smart, just like you. He had an idea. Down by the riverbank he found some reeds and cattails. Finding a long reed, he cut it in half with his knife and put it in his mouth. It was hollow, like a straw.

Then he waded into the river and lay down on his back. He hid beneath the water and stuck the hollow stalk above the water. He breathed through the stalk and stayed under the water where the wolves could not see him.

He stayed there for several minutes. He could hear the wolves howling at the edge of the water and splashing in the shallows. After a while, when they could no longer see or smell Daniel Boone, they gave up and trotted back into the woods.

Daniel waited until he was sure they had gone away, and

then he slowly sat up, looked around, and carefully—but quickly—hurried home.

Perhaps other storytellers will disagree: I don't feel a strong obligation to make sure the stories are historically accurate. If I did, I'd spend more time in libraries than I would spend actually telling stories. And, for young children, why clutter the anecdotes with footnotes? As long as the stories are presented as legends, as long as they're faithful to the general character of the historic individual, and as long as the story keeps the child's attention and offers a positive and satisfying conclusion, I've taken great liberties with the "historically based" tales I've told.

In this case, the purpose was not only to make the passing Kentucky woods more intriguing, but to make history come alive and to reinforce the idea that problems can be solved creatively. Someday, because of hearing about Daniel Boone's solution, my daughters might think up innovative ways to solve problems too.

This, of course, does have historical precedent. Many legends have grown up around the significant figures of history. Whether such legends are based on fact or an extension of an individual's reputation is difficult to tell. These stories, in fact, have become a bona fide genre themselves.

The life of Saint Francis of Assisi, for instance, spawned numerous stories. Here, adapted from *The Little Flowers,* is one such episode. Some have interpreted the story as a camouflaged narrative of Francis's encounter with a tyrant; Francis did rein in a despot or two, and some of these local strong men were as rapacious as wolves. Perhaps Gubbio was home to such a tyrant. Regardless, the story of the wolf communicates well with children and instills in them an appreciation for the courage and faith of Saint Francis.

The Wolf of Gubbio

Once while Saint Francis was staying in the town of Gubbio, the frightened townspeople told him of a ferocious wolf that lived nearby. The wolf was so terrible that it ate not only animals but men and women as well. The people were so frightened, they always carried swords or axes whenever they traveled. But even a sword or an axe wasn't enough if someone was alone on the road. So most people just locked their doors and stayed inside.

Saint Francis was known as a gentle man, but he was also brave. He decided to find the wolf. He did not carry a sword or an axe. He went out alone, trusting his safety only to God. A few people, who were afraid Francis would be killed, followed him to see what would happen.

Not far into the country, the wolf appeared with its teeth bared. Calmly Saint Francis prayed and said, "Come to me, Brother Wolf. I order you, in the name of Christ, do not harm me or the others." Immediately the wolf closed its mouth and came to the feet of Francis and lay down.

Then Francis said, "Brother Wolf, you have hurt and killed many people. The townspeople hate you and wish you were dead. But I want peace between you and these people. If you will stop hurting them, they will forgive you. Neither men nor dogs will pester you in the future. Do you promise not to hurt anyone ever again?" The wolf tamely lifted its paw and put it in Francis's outstretched hand.

The townspeople were amazed.

Francis told them, "Brother Wolf has promised not to hurt you, but he does need to eat. Do you promise to feed him every day?" The people happily agreed, and the wolf lived in Gubbio without hurting anyone and without anyone hurting him. Each day he went from house to house, and the people fed him. Before long, he was such a familiar sight that the dogs didn't even bark at him.

Finally, after two years, the wolf died of old age. The whole town was sad, because he had become their friend and had been a constant reminder of the gentleness and bravery of Saint Francis.

History's Stories

Encyclopedias, biographies and history books will provide an inexhaustible source of story ideas based on historical figures and incidents. Here are just a few names and events to get spark your own stories.

● Cyrano de Bergerac (1619-1655), a French author immortalized in Edmund Rostand's play as a witty romantic debilitated by his unusually large nose.

● Marie Curie (1867-1934), a Polish-born French physicist responsible for landmark discoveries involving radioactivity; a winner of two Nobel prizes.

● Oberammergau, a village in the Bavarian Alps which performs a Passion Play every ten years, fulfilling a vow villagers made in 1633 when they asked God to deliver them from the Black Plague—and the village was spared.

● "Grandma" Moses (1860-1961), a self-taught American artist who began painting at the age of seventy-six, winning international recognition.

● William Tell (14th century), a legendary Swiss hero who, as punishment for refusing to acknowledge Austrian authority, was forced to shoot an apple from his son's head with a crossbow—which he successfully did.

● Boston Tea Party (December 16, 1773), an incident in which American revolutionaries—in protest against Britain's high tea tax and import restrictions—dressed as Indians, boarded three British tea ships docked in Boston and threw the cargo of tea overboard into the harbor.

Story Starters

Here are some brief historic legends and sketches of historical figures that you can use as the basis for stories.

Joan of Arc

Long ago in the French countryside lived a young girl named Joan. Although she and her family were very happy, it was a hard time for France. Her country had been waging war with England for almost 100 years.

When Joan was twelve years old, she had a vision. She saw the Archangel Michael, Saint Catherine and Saint Margaret—and heard them speak to her. They told her that she was to help defeat the English and to help the rightful king of France take the throne. Because she didn't know how she could do these things, she told no one about the vision. Finally, when she was seventeen, Joan could keep her secret no longer. She told her older cousin.

Joan was so sincere that her cousin introduced her to a government official, who arranged for a trip to see Charles, the rightful king. After eleven days on horseback, much of it spent carefully crossing enemy territory, they reached Charles's castle.

First, Charles gave her several tests. Then he had his wisest advisers talk with her for many days. At last they all agreed that Joan was humble, pure and honest. She was officially put in charge of Charles's army.

Joan, wearing glistening white armor and riding a white horse, led the army to victory after victory. Thanks to Joan's successes, Charles was crowned King Charles VII of France.

Still Joan and her army continued to fight. During one bad battle, the French army retreated to a nearby fort for safety. When the commander thought the last soldier was safely inside, he raised the drawbridge, not realizing that Joan was still outside. Unprotected, she was surrounded and captured by her enemies. She was sentenced to death.

Joan was tied to a stake, and wood was placed around her feet and set afire. The people watching were silent. Then Joan cried out, not in pain but triumphantly, "Ah, my voices did not deceive me." Moments later she called out, "Jesus, Jesus," and then she died.

The English king's secretary, watching the flames, was the first to speak.

"We have killed a saint," he said.

Martin Luther

Long ago in Germany, a student was walking in the woods, when—crack!—a bolt of lightning struck very close by. Martin Luther was terrified. "Save me, Saint Anne, and I'll become a monk," he vowed.

He remained true to his promise. Martin joined a monastery, where he spent his time studying the Bible. But he wasn't happy. He felt guilty because of his unrighteousness, his sins against God. After many years, he read in the Bible that righteousness comes by faith, not by anything he personally could do. By trusting God, he was forgiven. His guilt was gone.

Because of what Martin had learned, he was very angry when he learned that a man named Johann Tetzel was making money by saying that sins could be forgiven by donating money to his church. Martin made a list of ninety-five reasons why such an idea was wrong. Martin nailed his list to the front door of a church, so everyone would read his words.

This got Martin in trouble with powerful men like Pope Leo and Emperor Charles V. He was forced to explain himself publicly. The emperor went so far as to threaten him with arrest. But Martin said, "Here I stand. I can do no other. God help me!"

On Martin's way home, men on horseback came galloping up to him and said, "You're coming with us!" Not knowing if they were friends or enemies, he allowed himself to be kidnapped and taken to Wartburg Castle. The men turned out to be friends, and they hid him in the castle so his enemies couldn't arrest him.

While living in the castle, Martin studied the Bible in Latin and translated it into German. Eventually he was able to return to his home, where he married, raised a family and became a teacher.

Florence Nightingale

When she was seventeen, a wealthy English girl named Florence Nightingale felt very strongly that she should serve people as a nurse. Her parents were shocked and angry. In those days, hospitals were filthy and dangerous places. The smells were so bad, they literally made people sick! But Florence had made up her mind. She traveled to different hospitals and learned how to be a nurse.

When many people caught the deadly disease cholera, lots of nurses refused to help, afraid they might get sick too. But Florence nursed the patients. When British soldiers went to fight the Crimean War, Florence was placed in charge of the nurses who went to care for the wounded.

Florence believed that hospitals needed good medicine, fresh food, pure water, and clean sheets and bandages—necessary things that were sometimes difficult to get or too expensive. She devoted herself to making hospital conditions the best they could be—and the wounded soldiers liked her because of it. They called her the "Lady with the Lamp" because, at the end of every day, she carried her lamp through the dark rooms of the hospital and visited all of them.

After the war, Florence returned to England and started a school for nurses. There she worked hard to pass laws that would make things healthier for everyone. Thanks to Florence Nightingale, hospitals are much safer places today.

These are just some of the interesting stories from history that can be adapted as stories for children. Encyclopedias, biographical dictionaries and even old textbooks will suggest a host of other possibilities. Too, when faced with an eager listener, you might be surprised how many forgotten incidents from history suddenly come to mind!

Chapter 10

Life Lessons

Stories help children feel at home in their ever-widening world. Through stories, children learn what to expect of the world and, in turn, what is expected of them. Stories allow children to take vicarious journeys into situations that could be theirs.

Melissa Heckler, a board member of the New York Story-telling Center, once described the special need that stories fill in the lives of children: "Stories talk about important values. We aren't taught about life's emotional adventures in school—stories prepare us for these emotional adventures. They teach about persistence, endurance, cleverness and kindness."

In addition, stories help children identify and strengthen their emotional and spiritual foundations. Along with the example of the adults they admire, the stories children are raised with are perhaps their most important moral influence.

One of the real advantages of storytelling is that it can be personalized to the needs of a child. "A story that's in a book is written for everybody," Heckler continues, "but a story that's told to you is just for you. Telling a story is real face-to-face communication."

Stories can help teach important lessons about life. Yet, because of the power of this face-to-face encounter, they should not become sledgehammers used to pound truth into ignorant and ornery urchins. Instead, stories should be seeds that implant concepts, attitudes, values and character traits which will prove fruitful in later years.

When a child disobeys or exhibits dangerous or self-destructive behavior, a story might be an effective way to show the logical consequences of that behavior. At such times, a story can be more effective than a stern lecture. However, for these stories to be most effective, they need to be planted before the stormy weather, not during the thunder and lightning of a confrontation.

It's better, for instance, to tell a story portraying the dangers of disobedience before—rather than after—confronting a rebellious child. Then, when a child behaves badly, you don't need to tell the story, the effect of which may be lessened because of the tension of the moment. Instead, you can say, "Do you remember the story of when Icarus disobeyed Daedelus?" or "Do you remember what happened to General Custer when he decided to do something foolish?"

Our goal is to teach children that values are personal choices, decisions they will have to make themselves. They will not always be popular or easy decisions, but stories can demonstrate that heroes rarely go along with the crowd.

To illustrate, one couple, Jim and Sally Conway, wanted to help their children understand the potential dangers of alcohol.

"We could tell our children not to drink because we don't like it, because the Bible says drunkenness is a sin, and because it's against the law for minors," said Sally. "But none of our reasons may be strong enough, however, when peers suggest drinking and parents aren't around to enforce the family position."

Instead, the Conways openly discussed the alternatives and their consequences—often with the help of a story (a newspaper article about someone driving under the influence, or personal knowledge of a family struggling with an alcoholic). Stories are a natural lead-in to a discussion that helps children form their own personal reasons for behavioral decisions—reasons that are more likely to endure even when Mom and Dad and other concerned adults are not around.

Teaching While We Entertain

Stories can vividly teach children about the world and how to live in it morally and responsibly. From Aesop to the Bible to Dr. Seuss, stories offer valuable life lessons and powerful images of right and wrong.

But a problem arises when we decide that a story's sole role is educational. Our stories become didactic lessons that almost certainly will fail to stir a child's imagination and sense of wonder about the world. Such stories become rules embroidered with character names.

Children are astute listeners. Although they often enjoy stories with concluding morals, they expect the journey to be as enjoyable as the destination.

Children give themselves over to stories in the hope of discovering a new world, meeting new people, participating in great adventures. If our stories are all of these things, children may remember the motivations and morals behind our stories for a lifetime.

Ideally, stories and family discussions about such tough issues need to start at least two years before children are confronted with the real thing. When milder topics are concerned, stories can be used after children face a specific life situation.

Here are some examples of the kinds of stories that teach life lessons—stories that can be used to instill good attitudes and character traits.

The Girls Who'd Never Seen an Apple Tree

One day, one of our girls was becoming extremely and exasperatingly opinionated. I didn't want to confront the situation straight on. Instead, I told the following story. It shows that we may not have all the facts just because we think we've seen something with our own eyes.

Once there were four sisters who had never seen an apple tree. Their names were Abby, Bonnie, Connie and Dawny [or any other four names that you can remember]. One day they asked their father where apples came from.

"From an apple tree," he said.

"What does an apple tree look like?" they asked.

"I'll show you," said their father. "But I'm going to show you one at a time."

The next day he took Abby out to see an apple tree. It was a cold winter day, and they walked through the snow to see the tree. It was just a scraggly, twisted trunk and limbs, bare and brown against the snow.

"That's an apple tree?" asked Abby in amazement.

"Yes," her father said. "That's an apple tree." And they went home.

A few months later, Father took Bonnie out to see the apple tree. It was spring, and a warm breeze was blowing. Bonnie looked and saw a tree covered with green leaves and small white blossoms.

"That's an apple tree?" asked Bonnie in amazement.

"Yes," said Father. "That's an apple tree." And they went home.

A few months later, Father took Connie out to see the apple tree. It was a hot summer day, and Connie saw a tree all covered with leaves and tiny, green fruit.

"That's an apple tree?" asked Connie in amazement.

"Yes," her father said. "That's an apple tree. Here, taste one," he added, plucking one of the small, green apples. Connie took a bite, and quickly spat it out! The fruit was so sour she couldn't even chew it. Then she and her father went home.

A few months later, Father took Dawny out to see the apple tree. It was early fall and the day was cool. Dawny saw a tree with bright red apples hanging from the branches.

"So that's an apple tree!" said Dawny in amazement. "Yes," said Father. "That's an apple tree. Here, taste one." Dawny took a bite. The apple was crisp, sweet and delicious. She ate the whole thing as they went home.

That night the four girls talked about apple trees.

"An apple tree is a strange tree," said Abby. "It doesn't even have any leaves—it's just brown."

"Oh, no," said Bonnie. "It's got leaves and lots of white flowers."

"It doesn't have flowers," said Connie. "It's got sour, green fruit."

"You're all wrong," said Dawny. "It's got sweet, red apples. I saw them!"

"Well, I saw the tree too," said Abby angrily. "It didn't have anything but brown branches."

The girls began arguing. Each of them said the apple tree was something different. Each girl insisted she was right and the others were wrong.

Who was right? [Some children will be able to answer, and their explanation will be a satisfying conclusion to the story. Others will need you to finish the story for them.]

To settle their argument, the four sisters went to their father. "Which one of us knows what an apple tree really looks like? Who's right?" they demanded.

"You all are," their father said. "The apple tree looks different at different times of the year. In the winter, it's brown and bare. In the spring, it's covered with leaves and white blossoms. In the summer, the blossoms turn into sour, green fruit. And in the fall, the fruit has turned into sweet, red apples. That's how an apple grows."

"You mean we all saw the same tree, but it changes the way it looks?" asked Abby.

"That's right. Just like you've changed the way you looked when you were a baby."

Dawny said, "I guess if we really want to know what an apple tree looks like, we have to look at it more than once."

All the sisters agreed. And they were right.

Lazy Tok

The peril of laziness is entertainingly presented by the story of Lazy Tok, which comes from *The Meeting Pool* by Mervyn Skipper, a collection of folktales from Borneo published in 1929. It continues to be a children's favorite. And the enjoyment is increased, I've found, if you present the Nipah tree branch-basket's words with a perky, lively voice and Tok's words with a lazy, drawling voice. It also adds to the effect if you close your eyes as you talk about Tok becoming so lazy that she eats with her eyes shut.

This is a story in which the dramatic pause can be used to great effect. When Tok insists that the Basket empty itself as usual, pause just before describing the Basket's actions. At the end, pause again as the children realize what has happened—and shudder with horror and pleasure.

The unfamiliar words in the story probably do not need to be explained beforehand. Most children accept them as part of the setting. However, a Nipah tree is an East Indian palm, a durian is a large, fleshy fruit, a pumelo is a kind of grapefruit and a Booloodoopy is whatever you might imagine him to be.

Once there was a creature named Tok, who was born lazy. When she was a baby, everyone said she was very good because she didn't cry, but really she was just too lazy to cry. It was too much trouble. The older she got, the lazier she got.

One day Tok was sitting on the riverbank, too lazy even to think about where her next meal was coming from, when the branch of a Nipah tree spoke to her.

"Good morning, Tok," said the branch. "Would you like to know how to get your meals without having to work for them?" Tok was too lazy to answer, but she nodded her head. "Well, tear me off the tree and I'll tell you," said the branch.

"That's too much bother," said Tok. "Couldn't you just shake yourself off?" So the branch shook himself hard, broke away from the limb of the tree and fell at Tok's feet.

"All you have to do to get your food is to make me into a basket," said the branch.

"What a nuisance," said Tok. "Couldn't you make yourself into a basket without my help?" So the branch made himself into a nice, wide basket.

"Good morning, Tok," said the Basket. "Would you like me to get your food for you?" Tok was too lazy to answer, but she nodded her head. "Then carry me and set me down next to the road," said the Basket.

"Do you think I'm a slave?" said Tok, yawning. "Couldn't you set yourself over by the road?" So the Basket picked himself up and laid himself down next to the road.

He hadn't been waiting long before a man from China came by and picked up the Basket. "What a nice basket! It would be perfect to put things in when I go to the market," he said. So he took the Basket to the market with him. Soon it was filled with rice, potatoes, pumeloes, durians, dried shrimps and other things too numerous to mention. But then the man saw a Booloodoopy, started talking with him, and set the Basket down. While the man was looking the other way, the Basket jumped up and ran away back to Lazy Tok.

"Here I am," said the Basket, "full of food. You only have to empty me out, and you'll have enough to eat for a week."

"What a bother," said Tok. "Couldn't you empty yourself out?"

"Very well," said the Basket cheerfully. And he emptied himself into Tok's lap.

Every week was the same. Whenever Tok ate up all the food, the Basket sat by the road, got himself carried to market and came back filled with pineapples and pumeloes and other nice things to eat.

Tok got fatter and fatter and lazier and lazier, until she was too lazy even to feed herself. The shrimps and the fruit had to drop themselves into Tok's mouth.

Then one day at the market, the man from China saw the Basket. "There you are, you thieving scoundrel! You're the one who's been robbing us." So he and his friends took the Basket and filled it full of soldier ants, lizards, spiders, bees, wasps, leeches, and all sorts of creeping, stinging and itchy things too unpleasant to mention. Then they let the Basket go.

Off ran the Basket, full of bugs and beetles and centipedes and gnats. It went straight home to Lazy Tok, who said, "What do you have for me today?"

"You'd better have a look," said the Basket. But Tok was too lazy even to open her eyes.

"I'm so tired, I couldn't lift a finger," said Tok. "Just empty yourself into my lap."

And so the Basket did.

Tok jumped up and ran and ran and ran. But the beetles and centipedes and lizards ran after her, and the wasps and bees flew after her, stinging and biting. The harder she ran, the harder they bit her. As far as I know, Tok is running still. But she is much thinner.

Chapter 11

Variety in Storytelling

After many retellings, even a favorite story loses its fascination for children. Don't let this call for variety take you by surprise; any storytelling technique, if overdone, will outlive its usefulness. It doesn't signal the end of your storytelling career. It *does* signal the need for fresh stories and new storytelling techniques.

There is no never-miss technique that will last forever, no in-depth preparation that will guarantee an endless stream of exciting stories. As Michael Phillips, a storytelling parent, advises: "Don't try too hard. I never plan out a week's stories for the family. Like the three princes of Serendip, we are just finding treasure along the way. However, like those picaresque princes, you have to be searching to find treasure."

Here are a number of ways to bring variety to your storytelling and, perhaps, discover greater treasure in the process.

Use Books to Tell Stories

Storybooks, of course, can be read to children, but don't feel confined to the printed page. The illustrations in many children's books can be a great stimulus for extemporaneous storytelling. The pictures become the jumping-off place for an impromptu story.

Young children, especially, can be enthralled without much of a plot. They simply enjoy identifying elements in a book's pictures. We can orient them to books—and stories—just by pointing out various details in the illustrations.

> "What do you see?"
> "Where's the cow's tail?"
> "Oh look, here's another ladybug hiding on the leaf."

Many wordless books, which are nothing but pictures that suggest a plot, are available. The responsibility for actually telling the story lies with the adult. This is a great way for beginning storytellers to develop their storytelling ability.

With slightly older children, we can use books to suggest ideas for our own story. One simple method is to substitute the child's name and the names of friends for various characters in the story.

When I retold "The Three Little Pigs," for instance, the pigs were renamed Stacey Pig, Kelsey Pig and Brian (a neighborhood friend) Pig. Whenever Kelsey Pig spoke, her line ended with a refrain that was familiar in our house: "... and where's my pacifier?" All of the children, including Kelsey, enjoyed this personalized version of a frequently told story.

Interlocking Stories

Occasionally you can surprise and delight your listeners by telling a story that connects with a previous story you've told. Earlier I briefly described the story of Fred and Frieda, the children who awoke to find their house filled with bubbles. Upon investigating, Frieda discovered that the bubbles were coming up through the drain in the bathtub. The story concluded with Frieda inserting the drain plug and rescuing her brother Fred, who had been scared by the invading bubbles.

The next night, I told about a turtle who enjoyed experiments. One day, he was swimming along and letting bubbles come out of his mouth. Then he found a pipe sticking into the lake. He wondered what would happen if he blew bubbles into the pipe. So he tried it. He blew and blew, and he never knew what happened to the bubbles. But my children did. They realized that those bubbles came out in Fred and Frieda's bathtub!

Some parents have enjoyed making up an ongoing story involving their child's favorite doll, pet or invisible friend, telling the further adventures of that character each night. Ideas for the story line can come from events of the day, childhood memories, or ideas and values that you want your child to understand. If you get stuck, ask your listener what would happen next. If you've picked a favorite character, the child is usually more than willing to let you know just what that character would do.

In addition to connecting the simple nonsensical stories we tell, an ongoing story line can be used with historical tales to help children see the interrelationships between people and events.

For instance, after telling the story of David, Goliath and the jealous King Saul, you can tell the story of Jonathan, Saul's son. In the second story, Jonathan meets David and admires him because he killed the giant Goliath. The two boys become close friends. The problem is that Jonathan's father, Saul, hates David and tries repeatedly to kill him. Jonathan's help is David's only hope for escape.

In this way, each story provides a context for the other. Children learn to see how the bits and pieces of life fit together. They also begin learning how to see the same events from a variety of perspectives.

Recording Your Special Creations

Children enjoy recording and replaying the original stories you (and they) tell. Capturing the stories on tape provides a great lasting memory for the future and makes a nice variation for an evening's storytelling.

Although a number of audio cassettes of children's stories are available, commercial tapes can't answer the questions a child inevitably wants to ask while a story's being told. If children are actively participating in a story that is being recorded, their questions and responses can become a permanent part of the tape.

I stumbled onto this technique one night after our family had been listening to commercial tapes. I had a blank tape available, so I thought I'd record a story for posterity. I pushed the record button as I began a meandering tale about an elephant who tried to give himself a shower by squirting water through his trunk. My daughter Stacey's questions became part of the story.

"Does it hurt to have water in your nose?" (Not for an elephant.)

"Did he have to use soap?" (No, elephants can't find soap big enough.)

"How about lotion?" (No, that's why elephants have such rough and wrinkled skin.)

"Was the trunk long enough to clean his whole body?" (Uh, good question...)

That night, Stacey wanted to hear the recording again and again. In fact, her normal request, "Can you tell another story?" wasn't forthcoming. She preferred to hear and re-hear the elephant story that she helped tell.

Acting Out the Story

One parent was having difficulty getting his toddler, Sarah, interested in stories. "She wouldn't sit still for stories," he said, "no matter what stories I told or how I told them. I had to think of some way to involve her. I decided we'd try acting out the story as I told it."

That night's story was about Jesus and a crippled woman mentioned in the Bible. Sarah became the woman.

"I explained that something was wrong with the woman's back. So Sarah, cloaked in a towel, walked around the room bent over and crying because she couldn't stand up straight. I played the part of Jesus. I put my hand on her back and said, 'Be well!' Immediately she stood up straight and began to shout, 'Hooray, I can stand up straight! Jesus healed my back!'

"We no longer had a problem keeping Sarah involved," concluded that father.

Our family enjoys acting out the story of Moses and the Israelites, who fled from Pharoah's army and crossed through the Red Sea. I tell how the Israelites are chased by Egyptian soldiers who want to take them back to slavery. The Israelites, running away as fast as they can, suddenly find themselves trapped! The Red Sea is in front of them, blocking their path. The soldiers are getting closer and closer.

At this point, my wife and I are on our hands and knees facing each other. We're the sea. The kids approach and one of them says, "We can't get across the water! The soldiers will get us." Another one, playing Moses, says, "Don't worry, God will save us." And Moses lifts up his arm. Just then the sea, Susan and I, raise our arms and wave them in the air. The kids quickly run through the "parted waters."

Then (and this is their favorite part) the kids circle around to play Pharoah's army. They try to go through the parted waters, and as they go through, the "waters" collapse on them, tackling them and wrestling them to the ground.

For children, the acting doesn't have to be theatrical. Simply getting them physically involved in the story is enough. You'll find that involving them physically will draw them in mentally and emotionally as well.

Guided Creativity

The most obvious variation on telling a story to your children is having your children tell a story to you. I frequently ask the children I'm with if they want to tell a story. Most often they'll say no. I don't insist; the purpose of storytelling is fun, not pressure. Occasionally they *are* willing to tell me a story. When that happens, I make sure their audience is appreciative and enthusiastic.

When children aren't ready to create their own stories entirely, we can guide them by providing the basic structure, letting them fill in the blanks.

> Once upon a time there were three little ____. And one day they decided to do something they hadn't done in a long time: ____. As they were getting ready, they suddenly were surprised to find that ____. "What will we do?" asked one of the little creatures. "I know," said another. "We can ____." So that's what they did. Yet it didn't turn out quite like they'd hoped. Something terrible happened, and they found...

This pattern of plan/problem/plan/problem can be repeated as long as the children enjoy filling in the blanks. For variety, ask them to decide key descriptions, decisions and details. When they (or you) run out of ideas, stop introducing further problems and obstacles. Let the next plan work exactly as they'd envisioned, thus concluding with a happy ending.

Besides fostering creativity, one of the benefits of this technique is that we get a glimpse into the child's mind. Patterns emerge in the way children answer. We can see better what they're thinking, what they like and what their natural tendencies are.

One of my coworkers encouraged his three sons to help tell original stories about such characters as Mortimer Mouse and Digger Dog. His oldest, Paul, would naturally turn the stories toward violent conflict. David, however, was more sensitive to people, and his stories were about characters who needed help and those who offered assistance. Joe sensationalized the story—everything was "the biggest" or "the strongest" or "the greatest."

Variety, for this father, meant encouraging his sons to broaden their horizons: "Paul, it's your turn to tell us what happens next, but the story can't be about killing." He helped them see things from a different point of view.

More Fill-in-the-Blank Stories

Using this technique, even the most familiar story outline can take on unexpected and exciting shapes.

Long ago in the land of ____, a mighty king was very upset when a ferocious invaded his kingdom and threatened his subjects. At first, the king tried to kill the beast with ____, but that didn't work. When a second attempt failed as well, the king turned to his wife, Queen ____, and asked for help. "Search our kingdom for a brave ____," she suggested. "Then..."

One morning, Janet was preparing to feed her pet ____ when it suddenly turned itself into a little girl. "Hello," the girl said. "I've been under a terrible curse. If we don't find the evil ____ who did this to me, I'll certainly become a ____ at midnight." Janet had planned to that afternoon, but she decided it would be more fun to...

Although Gerald had two sisters, he never liked to share his ____ with them. That was, not until he found the most wonderful thing ever, a ____. From that moment on...

Lisa was about to swat the fly with a rolled-up newspaper when it looked up and said, "____." Lisa couldn't believe her ears. She immediately wanted to tell her friend about it, but the fly stopped her. "Don't tell another soul," the fly said. "If you do, I'll surely..."

The Multiple-Ending Option

At times it's fun to start a story without knowing how it will end, leaving it up to our listeners to determine the story's conclusion. With this approach, we describe the setting, the situation and the dilemma. Then, when we get to the climax, we ask, "What do you think she did?" or "What happened next?"

If those questions elicit an "I don't know"—as they often do—I'll sometimes ask, "If you were there, what would you do?" No matter what the child says, my response is "That's exactly what she did." I then incorporate that answer into the story.

This technique works with adults as well as kids. Storyteller Fred Craddock tells of creating a story and asking his adult listeners to finish it—with unexpected results.

> There was a certain man who was very, very stingy. But as Christmas approached, some young people from a local church, not knowing him very well, asked if he would play Santa Claus in their program. In a moment of thoughtlessness and carelessness, he said he would.
>
> As the time approached, he grew nervous. The evening before the program, he said to his family, "Why in the world did they ask me? They know I don't go for all this Christmas cheer and gift-giving stuff. It's ridiculous. Why did they ask me?" He fussed and fussed, but he couldn't bring himself to back out on the young people at the last minute.
>
> Then he got serious and said to his family, "I hope you'll be thinking of me and praying for me so I'll do a good job even if I don't like the idea." His family said, "We will. And you will." So he went to the church with a Santa suit on, and it came to pass...

Then Craddock asked the people to come up with their own endings to the story. He let them think about it and discuss it. After a while he said, "Okay, how does the story end?"

A variety of possibilities were given, but finally one man suggested this ending: "And it came to pass that the stingy man was dramatically changed by his role as Santa. He realized what a tightwad he had become. He came home and began to give away all his wealth." The man paused. "And his family had him committed."

Extending Our Influence

Our children are with us only a short time. As parents, our job is to equip them for the time they will be on their own. We raise them to let them go. This "empty nest" some parents call freedom. Others call it grief.

We cannot live our children's lives for them; they have to face challenges in the future without us. We can send along only the values and virtues we've been able to instill. As one parent put it, "Good parenting is not so much the splash you make when you're around as it is the ripples that continue after you're gone." Stories, through the character traits they inspire, have a way of extending the ripples.

Although children can learn a great deal from stories—facts, impressions, attitudes—education is not the primary reason for telling stories. Stories can help unlock the imagination, which will serve a child well for a lifetime.

Imagination must be stimulated from an early age if a child is to keep from being confined to the narrow world of what can be seen and touched. Only with imagination can people envision a land never visited, partake in adventures they may never experience, understand another's life and, thus, develop compassion and appreciation for different ways of living.

Parent, pastor and storyteller Eugene Peterson's experience with a group of children illustrates the difference between an imagination nurtured and an imagination lacking.

"Thirteen four-year-old children sat on the carpet of the church sanctuary on a Thursday morning in February. I sat with them, holding cupped in my hands a last season's bird nest. We talked about the birds on their way back to build nests like this one and of the spring that was about to burst in on us.

"Winter was receding and spring had not quite arrived, but there were signs. It was the signs we talked about. The bird nest to begin with. It was weedy and gray and dirty, but as we looked at it, we saw the invisible—warblers on their way north from wintering grounds in South America, pastel and spotted eggs in the nest. We counted birds in the sky over Florida, over North Carolina, over Virginia. We looked through the church walls to the warming ground. We looked beneath the surface and saw earthworms turning somersaults. We began to see shoots of color break through the ground, crocus and tulip and grape hyacinth. The buds on the trees and shrubs were swelling and about to burst into flower, and we were anticipating and counting the colors.

"There are moments in this kind of work when you know you are doing it right. This was one of those moments. The children's faces were absolutely concentrated. We had slipped through the time warp and were experiencing the full sensuality of the Maryland spring. We were no longer looking at the bare nest; we were *seeing* migrating birds and hatching chicks, smelling the dewy blossoms."

Then the bearded and balding Peterson found the spell broken by one of the listeners, a youngster named Bruce who abruptly said, "Why don't you have any hair on your head?"

"Why didn't Bruce see what the rest of us were seeing?" Peterson wondered. "Why hadn't he made the transition to 'seeing the invisible' that we were engrossed in? All he saw was the visible patch of baldness on my head, a rather uninteresting *fact,* while the rest of us were seeing multi-dimensioned *truths*. Only four years old, and already Bruce's imagination was crippled."

It's no mortal sin, of course, for a four-year-old to be distracted by a fascinating detail. But Peterson's point is apt: Imagination is the capacity to make connections between the visible and the invisible, between past and present, between present and future. Children (or adults) who can't make those connections live in a confining world. Part of our job as parents and storytellers is to free our children from being prisoners of the present and the visible.

Without imagination we miss out on significant areas of life. Visualizing the unseen is an important part of daily existence. To understand a tree, for instance, we must "see" what we don't see at all—the underground root system which sends tendrils out through the soil, absorbing nutrients. We must "see" light pouring energy into the leaves. We must "see" the fruit that is now only a blossom.

These things can be seen only through imagination, something that children will need not only to understand trees, but to connect the material and the spiritual, the temporal and the eternal. Such imaginative vision is needed to develop invisible traits such as compassion, courage and foresight.

Imagination needs food, and stories provide many of the nutrients for this lifelong resource. Storytellers may think their work will soon be forgotten. But instilling an imagination lasts a lifetime. And, on a more modest scale, for many children a particular story often becomes a treasured memory for many years. Simply exposing children to good stories will have a lasting effect.

Long-time storyteller Eileen Colwell says, "I have told stories long enough to have had the experience of hearing an adult, once a child in one of my storytelling sessions, say, 'Do you remember that story you used to tell us as children? I have never forgotten it, and now I'm sharing it with my own children.' Through listening to stories, the child becomes aware of the magic and music of words. If the storyteller chooses wisely, her stories will awaken an appreciation of the great stories and traditional tales that are the heritage of every child.''

I hope you will find storytelling an equally rewarding experience. With a good story and a young listener, you cannot fail.